The Flower Girl

A COMPILATION OF SHORT STORIES

Betsy Munson

ISBN: 0615995292
ISBN-13: 9780615995298
Library of Congress Control Number: 2014906325
Betsy Munson, White Post, VA

DEDICATION

This book is dedicated to all of my family and friends who have encouraged me to write and to share my stories. To my friend and colleague, Clark Hansbarger, I am grateful for your encouraging words of support years ago when you read "Green Apple Girl." For my dear friends Sherri and Joy, I feel blessed every day for our lifelong friendship. To my daughter-in-law Yael, thanks for reading my stories and providing constructive criticism. For my sons Sean, Ryan, Clarke, daughter Misty, and daughter in law Renee, for their unconditional love and encouragement. To my two beautiful granddaughters, Indiana and London, for keeping the fun and laughter in my life. But most of all, this book is dedicated to my husband Steve, my love and my best friend, who has endured all of the late nights with the lights burning while I write.

TABLE OF CONTENTS

THE FLOWER GIRL

Next to the grime and grease of Joe's Garage is a vacant lot where a dilapidated green building stands with a sagging roof and a shaky floor. Although most people quickly pass the town's eyesore, a few walk slowly by. Some even stop, as if looking for someone or something they are missing and are in hopes of restoring, of finding again. In their memories are visions they cannot forget.

Of the people who stop and linger, one handsome man in his mid-thirties frequents this small plot of abandonment. Sometimes he appears to retrace steps he must have taken years ago. Other times, he brings a small bouquet of daisies or roses and places them atop unsightly weeds.

Years ago, in the middle of the small town, (right next to Joe's Garage and the only traffic light in the village), vibrant color and beauty were displayed under a canopy that was raised each morning promptly at seven a.m. and taken apart each evening at half past six. From this canopy, petunia baskets of velvety purple, fiery reds, vivid pinks, and subtle whites invited potential customers from the road. Festive impatiens of every color—salmon, lipstick pink, red, pale pink, lavender, and white—lured potential buyers under the shade to select lush plants in pots and hanging baskets.

By the roadside, the bright hues of yellow and orange marigolds mixed with bright-red salvia caught the attention of many passersby. On neatly stacked wooden tables, vegetable plants arranged in alphabetical order by variety were in packs of four and six. In between each

1

table of flowers or vegetables, small water fountains bubbled soothing sounds that suppressed the noise of nearby traffic. Miniature red and pink roses in full bloom outlined the green shed and invited customers inside. Hibiscus in pink, red, and orange framed the shed's windows, tempting shoppers to take them home.

Inside the shed, an old cash register was propped atop a tall counter. In the corner stood the only disorganized part of the shop: paperwork carelessly placed in stacks, invoices and a checkbook stub for anyone who cared to look. Although the linoleum floor was cracked and fading, the floor smelled of pine cleaner and was scrubbed daily. This establishment, The Flower Shoppe, became a haven of escape from the everyday tedium in the small town of Sunflower, Mississippi.

No one could pass The Flower Shoppe without at least admiring the floricultural beauty. But some remember this quaint little shop for the beauty who owned it. No one knew much about her. She wasn't from Sunflower County. In fact, no one really knew where she was from. She arrived one day at Joe's Garage in tight blue jeans and a red tank top in the spring of 1998. Joe heard the sound of her flip-flops as he turned to see the young woman standing in his waiting area. She was impatiently pushing her long blonde hair out of her face and walking nervously through the grimy room.

"Can I help you, miss?" asked Joe, wiping grease off of his hands with a white cloth.

"I'm inquiring about the lot next door that is advertised. It is for rent, isn't it?" the young lady politely inquired. "Can you tell me who owns it?"

"Well, ma'am, I'm the proud owner of the lot next door. But I don't rent it out to just anyone. I don't even know you. You new around these parts?" he asked.

"Yes, sir, I am. My name is Sarah...Sarah Bradley. I am honest to a fault. I pay my rent on time. As a matter of fact, I always pay in cash, up front. What are you asking for it per month?"

Joe eyed the girl up and down. He really didn't expect any takers for the dilapidated shed that adjoined his. Heck, he usually parked his junk cars in that lot. Sometimes the repair bill was worth more than the automobile, and the owners never showed up to claim their cars, leaving Joe with an eyesore of abandoned vehicles.

"I'm asking one hundred twenty-five per month to start," Joe said. He actually wanted two hundred dollars, but to get the chance to look at this beauty every day, he decided he'd take less.

"Well, my business is just seasonal. Bus I guess I would need to sign a year-round lease, right?" She rolled her eyes as if hesitating.

"Well, yes, I would need a year-round commitment. Now just what are you planning to do with the lot? You see– I've been catching a whole lot of grief from the town council on the looks of this place. But before we go any further, I need to know what kind of business you'd be conducting." Joe doubted if she'd be running a business that he could even agree to, but he figured he'd listen.

"Well, I think you are going to be surprised, Mr.....?"

"Porter...Joe Porter. I'd shake your hand, miss, but it's too greasy. I've been under the hood of that green Taurus over there."

Behind Joe was a lobby full of people. A bespectacled old man on a bicycle parked out front seemed to be listening to every word through the open door.

Well, Mr. Porter, everywhere I've been in business, they call me the Flower Girl. You'll have the prettiest spot in town after I get through. Oh, by the way, I'm handy with a hammer and a nail. But I might need a hand to fix that sagging roof. The shed there looks kinda dangerous. And if you don't mind, I'll be painting and fixing up the inside. The floor looks like it could use some linoleum."

Joe Porter chuckled to himself. "Well, now I'll still need an area right here to park cars."

Sarah looked in disgust. "Well, no wonder you're only charging me one twenty-five a month. I may as well bring a cart to display my plants. That's just a thin narrow strip."

"Well, ma'am, take it or leave it. But I've got a business to run and I need that spot."

"If you'd move some of those old junkers out of the way, I'd have more room, and the town council might get off your case. With what I'm gonna do with the little space I have, they're gonna love me. I'll fit right in with their beautification plan." Sarah didn't raise her voice, but she sure put Joe in his place.

Well, miss; first off, you'll need to get a business license. Why don't you go ahead and apply for that? Then come by tomorrow and I'll have the contract ready."

Sarah pulled out two hundred-dollar bills in cash. "That's my deposit. Just so you know I'm serious. I'll bring the other fifty when I come back tomorrow. You did want two months up front, right Joe?"

Joe would have been fine with any amount down as a deposit. He couldn't believe his good fortune. He had previously rented the lot to a craft company. They only lasted two, maybe three months, and he had only charged them a hundred dollars a month. But they had trashed up the place so much he had to evict them.

"Sure, that'll be fine, Miss Sarah. What did you say your last name was?"

"Oh, Joe, just call me Sarah, the flower girl. Everyone else does. I'll be by tomorrow afternoon, say around two?"

"That will be fine, miss."

Sarah Bradley left the lobby just as quickly as she had entered. Not only Joe, but everyone in the lobby turned and watched as she disappeared out of sight, down the corner and back toward the middle of town.

"Now, Joe, just what are you getting yourself into?" asked Beanie, the old man with the bicycle. He was always loafing around Joe's lobby. Beanie stroked his unkempt beard as he talked, stopping to take off his dingy glasses and wipe them with a dirty handkerchief. Joe let Beanie hang around in exchange for running errands around town when Joe got busy with customers. He could always pay Beanie with a fifth of cheap whiskey. The way Joe thought, it always paid to keep an alcoholic around. It kept his overhead down.

"Beanie, mind your business. I know what I'm doing. Right now, I need you to run across the street and get us a part for Mr. Ray's car. I promised him it would be ready this afternoon," said Joe crisply.

Beanie left the crowded lobby, mumbling under his breath. His tall, skinny frame appeared awkward, as he hopped on his bike and headed across the street to the auto parts store.

4

"You'd better watch out, Dad. First thing you know, Beanie will head to the liquor store before he gets back with that part," said Joe Jr. "Little Joe," as his dad fondly called him, was a senior in high school. Although Joe hoped that his son would go off to college, he was training him to take over the business, as a backup plan.

The next day, Sarah Bradley appeared at Joe's place around ten o'clock. She had on old blue jeans and a faded brown cotton shirt. Wearing work boots and a red bandanna holding back her long blonde hair, she looked ready to tackle the much-needed construction on the vacant lot.

"Here's the application for the business license, Joe. They tell me I should be approved within two days. I need this thing up and running 'cause I need the money," she stated.

Joe couldn't help staring at her. Even in her old clothes and with no makeup, she radiated beauty. Joe had his doubts that she could repair the place like she promised, but he didn't have anything to lose.

"Well, Sarah, what kind of tools do you need?" he asked.

"To start, I need a crowbar, hammer, and nails and some eight-foot studs to prop up that roof. I'm afraid the whole shed is gonna cave in when I start working on it."

"Well, that wasn't part of the deal. I'm not spending any money on that shed. You were supposed to be making all of the repairs."

"Yes, I agreed to do the repairs, but it's still your property. The way I see it, without me fixing up the place, it will soon be condemned. Is that really what you want? The way it is now, nobody can use it. Either get what I need or I just might complain to the town office about this being an unsafe work environment. Joe, you let me get injured because of that roof and I just might run you out of business," Sarah replied, her eyes flashing fire.

Joe looked down at the ground. He knew he was caught, as he had already taken her money and signed a contract. The town office had been trying to close down his unsightly repair shop for years. But he was grandfathered in even though the zoning laws had changed.

"OK, Miss Sarah," he said sarcastically. "I'll go and get you some lumber today at lunchtime. And I'll give you some tools, but that's it. The rest you'll have to do yourself."

"Wait a minute, Joe. I offered to do all of the repairs. But I told you up front I would need some help with the roof. Once we support the roof and stop the sagging, I will need some new shingles. And I'll need a small piece of linoleum for the floor."

Joe just smiled and walked away. He'd buy the lumber. But he was not going to buy new shingles or linoleum right now. He'd wait and buy some at an auction. After he paid his help and mortgage, he rarely had extra money.

Sarah spent the next two days clearing the lot and repairing the shed. The loafers and people getting their cars repaired spent most of the day watching Sarah as she methodically carried trash bags to the bin. After the lot was cleared to her approval and Joe bought the necessary lumber, she propped up the shed and began the repairs, replacing old, worn boards, rusty door hinges and knobs.

After two days of hard work, the lot began its major transformation. Sarah painted the weathered shed a dark green. She made Joe move some of his old cars out of her lot and cleared all of the trash and debris. With some sealant, she fixed the roof's leaks and replaced boards and posts to make her shop a safe haven for potential customers.

The renovations did not go unnoticed by the townspeople. Members of the town council smiled and spoke encouraging words to Sarah as they briskly walked by. Two elderly ladies stopped by to say hello. Sarah noticed they were identical twins.

"It's so nice to see the place cleaned up. What kind of shop is this gonna be?" asked one twin.

"A flower shop. I'll start bringing in my plants tomorrow. Please come by and browse," Sarah replied politely.

"Well, we'd love to. But we don't have much money. We live on a small pension. But we'll definitely come by," replied the other twin.

The ladies left as quickly as they came in, heading toward the center of town. Sarah later saw them when they returned with packages from the Dollar Store and the pharmacy. Sarah waved as they smiled and walked on.

Sarah wished she had asked the ladies' names. She always tried to learn customers' names as soon as possible. Small businesses were tough to get started. Just remembering names sometimes created impulse sales.

As promised to the elderly twins, Sarah arrived the next day in her old van loaded with plants, pallets, and cinder blocks. Building her display tables from the cinder blocks, she methodically decided where the flowers would be displayed. Like an artist with a blank canvas, and using a palette of complimentary colors, Sarah slowly arranged her lush green plants, choosing specific colors for certain tables. One table appeared patriotic with sections of red, white, and blue petunias. Other tables contrasted white and various colors of impatiens, while solid colors of marigolds made a skirt around the makeshift tables, creating color from the ground up.

Joe came over at lunchtime to compliment Sarah on what she'd accomplished.

Holding a sandwich in his greasy hand, he smacked his lips together while eating his hamburger.

"Nice job, Sarah," he muttered as he licked mustard off his fingers. "Want a burger?"

"No, thanks. I brought my lunch. I'm actually not much on eating meat anyway. But thanks for the offer."

"Are you one of those weird vegetarians?" asked Joe.

"Well, does it really matter, if I pay my rent on time?" snapped Sarah.

"No, I guess it doesn't. I didn't mean to offend you. By the way, I'm going to an auction this weekend. I'm gonna try and buy enough shingles to fix the roof. I'll get someone to help you with that. And I'll try and find some linoleum for your floor," he replied.

Sarah smiled. "Joe, I really appreciate that. You help me a little and I'll help keep the town council off your back. Now, if you'll excuse me, I have to get back to work."

Every day for a full week, Sarah arrived promptly at seven a.m. in her van loaded with beautiful plants. It was late February; so many people looked but didn't buy. The planting season usually began in full swing the first week of March.

The last Saturday in February, Sarah arrived at the shop holding a little girl's hand.

Joe noticed the little girl and strode into Sarah's shop.

"Sarah, it's obvious this is your daughter. She's the spittin' image of you. But I don't want her around this shop. Sometimes the guys I work here…well, their language gets pretty rough. It's not what you want for a little girl. And it's so close to a busy road. How can you watch her and work?"

"Well, Joe, it's like this. I've given you two months rent. I also have to pay my house rent and food. And my business won't start to bring in money until next week. I can't afford to pay a babysitter for another weekend. Your boys will just have to tone it down while we're here. By the way, that crude language doesn't exactly sit well with your customers, either. That's what I've been hearing from people stopping by. If you want to stay in business, you'd better be a boss and make them clean up their language. And by the way, that bathroom we have doesn't work right. Every time we use it, the commode keeps running and floods the concrete. Lucky it's not attached to the shed. So, I guess we'll have to come over and use yours. So I would appreciate if you take down that calendar of the naked girl. I don't want to have my daughter see Miss February showing her tits for all to see."

Joe just looked at her and shook his head. But by the end of the day, the calendar featuring Miss February was in the trashcan.

A few weeks passed, and Sarah had plenty of townspeople admiring her flowers, but she had few buyers. Yet each morning she arrived promptly and arranged her flowers on the pallets with her little girl, Molly, helping on the weekends. She carefully watered her plants whenever they dried, and fertilized them twice a week, so every plant had lush dark-green foliage.

One morning, a middle-aged man donning a white cowboy hat and heavy black glasses arrived at her shop.

"Miss, I run errands for all of the businesses. Can I get you coffee or doughnuts?"

Sarah looked at him more intently. She could barely understand his broken, tongue-tied words.

As he approached her, Sarah noticed how he walked with a noticeable limp. Part of her pitied him and another part of her wanted him to leave and never return. She sure couldn't afford to buy coffee and doughnuts every day.

"No, thank you, sir," she replied.

"What's your name?" asked the man, turning his head in a curious childlike fashion.

"Sarah," she replied, and turned, pretending to pick dead leaves off her petunia plants.

"Everybody calls me Tex, 'cause I like to wear cowboy hats. I used to live out west. But my wife died and I moved here," he replied. "I'll be downtown every day except Sunday. If you need any errands run or need food at lunch, just let me know."

"Sure, I'll keep that in mind," Sarah replied halfheartedly. Something about this man gave her the creeps. From the looks of him, he never had a girlfriend, much less a wife. She watched Tex as he limped down Main Street and entered the First National Bank lobby. Sarah felt lost and alone, with no friends, in a little town where everyone knew everyone's first name. Everyone's name except Sarah Bradley's.

By the beginning of March, Sarah had her little shop stocked heavily for the spring season. Business started to increase. Practically everyone who worked downtown browsed through her plants and purchased something. Most of the sales were small, a single tomato plant or a pack of annuals. But every sale added up.

The first weekend in April was Easter weekend. Sarah left her daughter with a baby-sitter, expecting good sales. As usual, Tex came by wanting to run errands for her, and, as usual, he quickly disappeared when she refused his offer.

Business was brisk that day, her biggest day of the season. The cash register was ringing, and sales were steady all day. Couples and families with children browsed through her small shop, filling flats full of colorful flowering plants, while others purchased small trees or verdant tropicals. At the end of the day, she was exhausted, but she left her shop with a smile on her face. Today she had enough money in her pocket to pay the back rent she owed on the little house she rented by the railroad track. With today's sales, she could pay her past-due electricity bill to avoid an interruption in service.

Sarah picked up Molly from the baby-sitter, with an important announcement. "Mol, we're going to the store. And you can help me pick out the food you want," she exclaimed.

"No more rice for every meal, Mommy?" asked Molly.

"Not this week. We can have milk and cereal in the morning. And we can buy hot dogs or hamburger meat and definitely chicken tenders, your favorite."

Sarah was so tired from her workday that shopping for groceries was difficult. But she managed to make it fun for her daughter, who picked out not one but two types of sugary cereal and three types of candy.

Darkness was falling when mother and daughter arrived at their small house. A train whistled in the distance, and Sarah busied herself putting away the groceries, while Molly played with a dilapidated doll in the center of the living room floor. After dinner, she helped Molly with her bath and tucked her into bed.

"Mommy, how come we keep moving from town to town?" asked Molly, her long blonde hair falling around her face. "I sure did like the town we lived in last year."

Sarah caught her breath and contemplated her reply.

"I know it's been hard on you moving from place to place. I am looking for the perfect place to raise you, and I haven't found it yet. When I do, you and I will both feel right about it," she responded.

"And why did Daddy leave us? I miss him so much. If he wanted to come back to us, how would he know where we are?" Molly asked. She was only six, but the hard times she'd lived through made her wise beyond her years.

Sarah was used to this question. Molly asked it from time to time. Although Sarah tried not to miss her old boyfriend, nights like tonight made it difficult to forget how lonely it was raising a child without a father.

"Your father…well, he loves you and me. He just had a hard time with settling down," Sarah lied. She didn't want her daughter to know that she and Wayne never planned a family. Wayne made it clear to Sarah he never wanted children.

After Molly was born, he threatened to leave many times, but Sarah kept believing he loved her enough to stay. But two weeks before Molly's fourth birthday, Sarah found a note from Wayne saying he couldn't take it anymore and he was moving on. She waited through the fall and summer months, operating a successful flower shop in Atlanta, hoping every day he'd change his mind and come home. But by fall, it was pretty evident he'd never be back. At the time, Sarah was twenty-four and doing her best to raise her daughter with some help from her mother and sister. But memories of Wayne and happier days surrounded her with sorrow. She knew she had to leave or, unlike Wayne, she would never move on.

So she packed all of her possessions and left after the Christmas season.

"Just what will you do now?" asked her mother. "I know what it's like to raise children on my own."

"I'll be OK. I just have to break away for a while, Mom. I can't keep depending upon you and Sis," she replied. "Beside, I can't stand the memories of Wayne. They're everywhere here," she replied. "Don't worry. I'll be back to see you at Thanksgiving and stay until the New Year. That is, if you'll have Molly and me for that long."

Her mother burst into tears. "You know you're welcome here, dear. I don't have much. Lord knows it's hard living off the pension I have from you dear father, God rest his soul. But we'll make do."

As her mother kissed Molly good-bye, Sarah hugged her sister, Gracie, for one last time.

"You know, it kills me to see you go. You had better write me when you get to your new place." Gracie wiped a tear from her eye.

"I will, Gracie. I promise." Then she and Molly drove away from Atlanta, as her mother and sister waved in the distance.

The next growing season, Sarah rented a little shop she discovered in Baton Rouge, Louisiana. Sarah made a profit during the spring season. But summer was one of the wettest seasons on record. Thunderstorms came out of nowhere. Her little shop was pelted with high winds and rain day after day. Plants were damaged by the wind and many succumbed to excessive water, literally rotting in their pots. Sarah took this as an omen she shouldn't stay in Louisiana. That fall, she closed up shop and waited tables at a local seafood restaurant. In the evenings, she cared for Molly and tried to keep busy. But late at night, she missed Wayne. She thought of how he would smell after he showered. Or how he would gaze at her as they lay in bed together, their bodies seeming to merge into one.

A few guys asked her out, but each time, she refused. She was hanging on to something she didn't have anymore. And even in this town, Wayne's memory overshadowed everything she did.

Yet Molly seemed happy in this little town. They rented a tiny upstairs apartment, from a kind, retired widow, Mrs. Connelly. When Sarah worked, Mrs. Connelly watched Molly at no charge. Mrs. Connelly had a granddaughter close to Molly's age, who visited often. So when Sarah arrived home one day from the restaurant and broke the news to Mrs. Connelly that she and Molly were moving, Mrs. Connelly was stunned.

"Dear, why on earth would you move that child from here? She seems so contented."

"Mrs. Connelly, I can't explain it. But something just isn't right about this place. When I get to the right place, I'll know. Molly and I will miss you greatly. I'll write when I get to the next place. Please keep in touch," Sarah replied, leaving Mrs. Connelly's immaculate apartment for the last time.

Sarah and Molly departed in the middle of the night. Knowing Molly would cry when they left, Sarah gently carried Molly to her old van and laid her down on the back seat. Molly sighed but did not awaken. With tears in her eyes, Sarah cranked up the dilapidated van and off they drove in the dark, with no real plans on where they'd set up shop again. But as Sarah drove, fighting off sleep through the night, she was determined the next town would have what she was looking for. The only problem was, she really didn't know what it was she wanted. And even worse, if she found it, she didn't know if she'd see it for what it really was.

Sarah drove the four hours to the Mississippi border. Seeing a rest area, she stopped for a few minutes to let Molly run around, and to collect her thoughts. A wave of panic swept over Sarah. Tucked inside a small plastic jar contained her life savings—nine hundred dollars and some change. Quickly, she had to find a small town where she could display her talents and her flowers.

Looking at a faded map, she decided to take Route 3, which would lead her through Sunflower County and right through the center of Sunflower. As she traveled through the small Southern towns, no site seemed appropriate, or available. But the minute she stopped at the traffic light in Sunflower, she saw the vacant lot for rent and envisioned what it could become under her care.

The old house she found to rent in Sunflower was a shabby wooden cottage on the edge of town. Paint was peeling off every room and the rugs were stained. Sarah planned to repaint the dingy walls when she had the time and money. A rusted screen door in the back led to a spacious yard with room for a garden and a swing set for Molly, which Sarah hoped to buy with her spring profits.

———

The last weekend of April was still a busy time for Sarah's shop. On Saturday, Sarah took her daughter to the baby-sitter at six o'clock in the morning. Although she didn't open until nine, she wanted to arrive early. She needed any extra money an early-bird shopper might be willing to give her. At eight o'clock, a few people were browsing through the neat rows of bedding plants. Most were "just looking," but she did manage a few sales. Around eight thirty, Sarah dragged the garden hose through the rows of plants to refresh the plants that had dried from the steady wind. Suddenly, she heard footsteps behind her. She turned to see a tall young man standing there gazing over her plants. She cut off the water and strode over to assist him.

"May I help you, sir?" she asked in her best professional voice.

"Yes, ma'am. I need a gift for a special lady who loves plants," he replied.

His voice was soft, yet direct. Sarah found herself running her hands through her hair and wondering how she looked. To her dismay, patches of dirt were on her jeans, and sweat was already trickling down her back.

"Well, I would recommend the assortment baskets. They have a mixture of petunias, sweet alyssum, lobelia, and geraniums. I arrange and plant them myself in large wire baskets. Would you like to see them?" she asked.

"If they are created by you, by all means, I'd love to see them," he replied softly. Then he looked her straight in the eyes, a wide smile growing across his chiseled face. "I'm Jonas—Jonas Baker. I've been admiring your shop for several weeks and have been planning to stop by. Today, I was driving past and decided to come in."

"I'm Sarah Bradley, the owner of this humble establishment," she responded. He was so handsome that her eyes kept averting his. She was afraid she'd start stuttering and forget she needed to sell him as much as she could. She desperately needed the money.

"Let me show you what I call my "collection baskets," because I sort of throw all sorts of different plants together. It seems to work. They're one of my best sellers."

Sarah waved her hand, and Jonas followed her through the rows of plants. Other customers were browsing. Sarah greeted them but continued to assist Jonas. She couldn't seem to focus on anything or anyone else.

Jonas asked Sarah questions about every plant that caught his eye.

"This lady must be really special," Sarah uttered softly, hoping Jonas didn't hear.

"You have no idea. And like yourself, she really loves plants," he replied, waiting to see Sarah's response.

Sarah's smile faded. This was the first time she felt attracted to a man since Wayne. But now she knew Jonas was already spoken for.

Jonas carefully examined one of Sarah's largest hibiscus plants, before selecting two hibiscus plants with double orange blooms. "OK, I've spent a fortune here. I need to wrap this up, or I won't be able to get them all home."

Sarah calculated Jonas had already spent more than a hundred dollars—maybe a hundred and fifty. She was worried he'd put some plants back when he found out the total.

"I also need some plants for cutting flowers. What do you recommend? The lady I have in mind would love to have her flowers in vases on the table. But I'm bad at this. And I really want to impress her. Please pick out something you think she would like. She shares your love of flowers."

Jonas listened intently to Sarah's recommendations, his lean frame edging closer to Sarah. She smelled his cologne and wanted to be drawn into his arms.

Sarah selected three rosebushes —one covered with white buds, one blush pink, and one rose pink.

"If you want to impress her, cut a flower from each rose and wrap them in bright pink paper. One rosebud stands for yesterday, one for today, and one for tomorrow."

"I'll remember that. Now, Sarah, I've taken enough of your time. You have plenty of other customers to attend to. How much do I owe you?" he asked.

Sarah scanned the wagon full of plants and totaled up his order. He had spent nearly two hundred dollars, more than she'd ever sold to a single customer.

Jonas pulled out two crisp one-hundred-dollar bills and a crumpled twenty.

"Sir, I don't think you understood. You owe me one hundred ninety-six dollars and some change." She grasped the twenty and extended it toward his open hand.

"No, that's for you, for your help," he said.

Sarah shook her head adamantly. "Sir, I don't take handouts."

"Jonas…call me Jonas. And it's not charity. I don't want it back."

"Well, thank you, thank you so much," she replied. "And Jonas, please come back."

"Oh, don't worry. I may need a few more plants. What time do you open on Sunday?"

"At noon. I work seven days a week. I need to sleep in once a week," she replied.

"I might see you tomorrow," said Jonas. "See you, Sarah. So nice to meet you."

"The feeling's mutual," said Sarah as she shook his hand. His handshake was firm, and she somehow felt protected by his strong grip.

As abruptly as he had appeared that morning, he disappeared. Sarah watched as he vanished in a black sports car, loaded with her plants. She sighed, trying to forget about Jonas, and began assisting the other customers who waited patiently.

At the end of the day, Sarah had over five hundred dollars in her moneybox. It had been her most profitable day so far. She was exhausted from an entire week of hard labor, but she knew she had to find some energy for Molly.

That evening, as she and Molly ate leftover Hamburger Helper and baked potatoes, Sarah pretended to listen to her daughter. But she kept thinking of Jonas. She kept seeing his handsome slender physique following her around the shop. As she thought of embracing him in a passionate kiss, all realities of paying bills and working seven days a week to care for her daughter were swept away.

"Mommy, you haven't heard a word I said," shouted Molly, her lips drawn in a pout.

"Sorry, honey, I just had a really tough day. Let's watch some television...your choice. I'll make us some popcorn."

"Mommy, I don't like it here."

"Why, where did that come from? You just have to give it some time," replied Sarah.

"I miss Grandma and Mrs. Connelly. And I really haven't made any friends at school."

"I know it's been hard moving around like we have. Don't worry. Just give it some time."

Sarah clutched her daughter to her chest and still thought about Jonas. She knew he must belong to someone else and she shouldn't think about him. But the thought he might be back in her shop tomorrow made her heart race.

The next morning, Sarah awoke at eight o'clock and lounged around the house in her pajamas as she prepared pancakes and juice for Molly. She dropped Molly off at the sitter's house at eleven o'clock and drove through the tranquil town to the flower shop. A few people were already browsing through her flower displays.

As she approached the green shed to open the register, she saw three rosebuds propped against the doorstep wrapped in pink paper...one white, one pale pink, and one dark pink. On a card attached to the pink paper was a note: "To Sarah. For yesterday, today, and tomorrow."

Sarah placed the roses in a small refrigerator and tried to concentrate on her duties in the shop. Anger welled inside her. Why had he teased her with these flowers when he was involved with another woman?

At noon, she saw him out of the corner of her eye. He was walking straight toward her, his eyes only on her.

She attempted to ignore him by asking all of the browsing customers if they needed assistance. When they declined her offer for help, she started picking dead leaves off the geraniums, pretending not to see him.

After waiting a few minutes, Jonas spoke out loud. "Excuse me, miss. I need some assistance. There are several flowerbeds at my house in need of some color. Can you assist me?"

"I'd be happy to help you. But why didn't you bring your wife to help you pick them out?" she snapped back.

"Well, I'd love to oblige, miss. But she up and left with my banker about three years ago. Ask anyone in town," he replied as he walked toward her.

Sarah blushed in embarrassment for assuming anything about Jonas's personal life.

"And who might the special lady be that you bought the plants for yesterday?" she asked.

"The one and only woman in my life right now…my mother. I must confess. I'm a momma's boy."

Sarah wanted the concrete to open up and carry her away from this embarrassing moment. But as that wasn't an option, she turned toward him.

"You've been so busy assuming things that you haven't mentioned the flowers. Do you still have them, or did you toss them in the trash?" he asked.

"Oh, I have them. They're in a safe place so I can enjoy them when I get home. I have a perfect vase for them. Thanks so much. And I—I'm so sorry I made a false assumption yesterday. But you did say the flowers were for a special lady," she argued.

"And my mother sure is that. Raised me well after my father died when I was fifteen," he added. "But enough about me. You already know more about me than I know about you. I do need more bedding plants for my house and my mom's." He rolled up his sleeves. "Let's get to work."

Sarah made suggestions to Jonas based on how much sun his flowerbeds received. And whatever Sarah suggested, Jonas bought. He also purchased two more hibiscus plants for accents, the most expensive plants Sarah sold.

This time his bill totaled over four hundred dollars.

"Jonas, I don't want to be taking all of your money. You've spent a fortune with me. But I do appreciate it. I have a daughter at home depending upon me."

As she handed him his change across the counter, his hand grazed her wrist ever so lightly. "So, is there a Mr. Bradley waiting for you at home? You're not the only one out on a limb here," he said.

"No, no Mr. Bradley. Just my daughter and me."

"Well, I know you've had a rough week. How about if I take you and your daughter out for a burger? Or better yet, you could come to my place and I could whip something up for you. Since my wife left me, I've become a pretty good cook."

"Oh, I don't know. Molly has school tomorrow."

"Well, I could have something ready as soon as you close. That would save you from cooking. I sure could use some company. Besides, I have to plant all of these plants at my house as well as cut my mother's grass today. It would be nice to have some company after all that."

"OK, I close up at five. What about if we drop by around six?" replied Sarah, wondering why she was saying yes, but deep down knowing why. Jonas had the most beautiful green eyes that softened every time he looked at her.

Jonas wrote down the directions to his house and his phone number on one of her sales slips and waved off her help as he made several trips to load the plants in a white pickup truck.

At five, Sarah promptly closed up shop and raced to her van. She hastily picked up Molly from the sitter.

"Mommy, why are you in such a hurry? I didn't get to tell Miss Jean good-bye."

"Well, a new friend of mine invited us to dinner. So let's go home and get cleaned up and go. We don't have to cook tonight."

"Is it Daddy? Is he in town?" Molly's blue eyes brightened.

"No. His name is Jonas."

"Oh," said Molly. Disappointment filled her eyes.

"Well, I think we can have some fun tonight," said Sarah. A smile lit up Sarah's face that hadn't been there for years.

As Sarah drove the short distance to Jonas's house, Jonas was busy preparing steaks on the grill, baked sweet potatoes, and a tossed salad. As a bachelor, he sometimes ate frozen dinners or opened up cans of food. But tonight was special.

When Sarah arrived, some blues music was playing in the background. She recognized the melodic voice of Nina Simone.

As they ate their meal, Sarah noticed the sour look on Molly's face. No matter how hard Jonas tried to converse with Molly, she answered tersely or ignored him.

Sarah tried to enjoy her meal, but it was difficult when she observed how rude her daughter was to Jonas.

After Jonas finished his meal, he offered Molly some ice cream, but she just shook her head no. There was a deep longing on Molly's face, as if she expected her father to walk through the door any minute.

"Molly, I have a friend of mine I think you should meet," Jonas announced.

Molly tried to ignore him, but curiosity was beginning to waiver her stubborn resistance to Jonas.

"What friend? I don't see anyone else here," said Molly.

"Well, she's kind of shy, especially now that she's had a family. But we need to be quiet so we don't frighten her."

Molly followed behind Jonas, tiptoeing past the kitchen and through a metal door that led to the screened porch on the back of the house. Inside a cardboard box lay a gray cat with four multicolored kittens. Molly squealed in delight as Jonas picked up a kitten for her to hold.

That night, Sarah and Jonas sat on the porch conversing, while Molly watched cartoons. When Sarah later checked on her daughter, Molly was asleep on the couch, a kitten tucked under her right arm.

As Sarah kissed her sleeping daughter on the cheek, she could feel Jonas's eyes following her every move. Suddenly, she felt her cheeks flush.

Desire stirred within her, desire she thought would never be rekindled. Right then, that night, she knew she wanted Jonas. As these thoughts raced through her mind, she tried to ignore them. She didn't have time or energy for a relationship. Her main responsibilities were to run her shop and to take care of her daughter. But deep inside, she wanted to take roots in this town and settle down.

Walking back into the living room, Jonas motioned for her to sit down on the couch, next to him.

"Thanks for a nice evening. I can't remember the last time I had this much fun," sighed Sarah.

"You're welcome, my dear lady," replied Jonas. He gently turned her face toward his and kissed her lips softly, tenderly. Sarah put her arms around him and stroked the hair that had fallen across his forehead.

"I really need to be going. I have to be at work early," Sarah said.

"You could always stay here tonight." Jonas smiled and winked.

"In your dreams."

"Yes, every night since I saw you set up shop in Sunflower," he quipped. "But I have to work tomorrow, too. I have to draw up house plans for a new client. But if you must leave, I'll help you with Molly."

Jonas carried Molly to the van and laid her down on the back seat.

"Thanks for dinner," said Sarah.

"Any time. How about this Friday? How about dinner and a movie?"

"I'll think about it," replied Sarah. "Why don't you drop by the shop one day this week? I would love to hear how all of your plants are doing."

"Well, if I have any problems, I expect a home consultation from the expert. After all, I have to be your best customer."

"That you are. No one else comes even close," she murmured. Then she gave him a quick kiss on the cheek and jumped in the van. "'Night, Jonas. See ya."

"Good-night, Sarah. I'll stop by one day this week." He watched as she pulled out of his driveway and disappeared from sight.

Sarah didn't see Jonas on Monday or Tuesday. On Wednesday morning, she felt certain she would see him stroll into her shop before closing. But she busied herself with several customers waiting for her to open for business.

Around eleven o'clock, the rush was over and Sarah was watching the clock, hoping she could eat her lunch without being interrupted. As she tidied up her office, an elderly black man entered the shop.

"Excuse me, ma'am, but I sure could use your help with buying some flowers. Do you have any red geraniums?"

"Yes, sir. I have some lovely ones. Would you like to see them?"

"Well, yes, but I need some other flowers, too." He pulled a crumpled piece of paper from his pocket. "I need some hanging baskets. Two with white impatiens and one with pink begonias. Oh, and I need some sweet alyssum."

"I can help you with everything on your list," said Sarah. She picked out the gentleman's flowers while he stood and watched under the shade of the shed's overhanging roof. As he waited, he pulled a handkerchief from his pocket and wiped beads of sweat from his forehead. He was dressed in faded jeans and work boots. But his hands were what caught Sarah's eye. His large, weathered hands knew the stress of hard labor.

Sarah pulled a red wagon filled with the man's flower requests and parked it right next to him.

"Will there be anything else for you, sir?" she asked. "And do these meet your approval?"

"Yes, yes, they'll do just fine. I'll be back next week for some tomato plants."

Sarah waved him inside to the cash register. When she had his bill totaled, he pulled out three crisp twenties and handed them to her. When she handed him his change, he paused and turned his head, gazing at her for a few seconds.

"Ma'am, I have to work hard for my money, and when I come home I'm dead tired. But I buy these flowers to honor my wife's memory. I'm going to take them out to her gravesite. She loved her flowers. Took care of those flowers until the cancer took over her body. The day before she died, I rolled her bed out on the front porch just so she could see the roses and petunias in full bloom." The old man paused as tears rolled down his cheeks. "Now don't you worry, miss. I'll take care of these flowers. I'll do my best to keep them pretty. If these don't do so well, I'll be back for more."

Sarah felt tears welling up in her eyes. She fought hard to keep her composure. Customers frequently chatted with Sarah, but no one had ever shared a personal loss in this manner. The elderly man's pain was palpable.

"Sir, you must have loved her very much. You must miss her greatly."

"Only every minute of every day, miss," he replied.

"Call me Sarah. And would you mind giving me your name?"

"I'm Frank Baltimore. Nice to meet you, Miss Sarah. I'll be back next week to get my vegetable plants. See you then." He slowly walked outside into the Mississippi heat, carted off his plants, and disappeared from sight.

But all day long, Sarah thought about Mr. Baltimore's devoted love for his deceased wife. And she longed to have in her life what Mr. Baltimore knew… unconditional love. She thought about Jonas and wondered if she and Molly could build a future here with him.

———

The summer heat came early in Mississippi. And when it arrived, people stopped buying plants and started planning summer vacations and trips to the swimming pool. Sarah kept her hanging baskets and larger plants in stock and brought in freshly cut flowers in hopes of keeping a positive cash flow. This season had been one of her most successful, thanks to many devoted customers like Mr. Baltimore, who came every week to buy new flowers for his wife's grave. The week she began stocking fresh flowers, he bought a huge arrangement of sunflowers and white daisies to bestow upon his wife's plot. Sarah continued to marvel at this man's devotion to his deceased wife.

But her best customer by far was Jonas. Every Friday, he purchased cut flowers from her, swearing they were for his mother. Before noon each Friday, he would buy different arrangements—sometimes pink roses and baby's breath, and other times, burgundy freesias and blue delphiniums. And every Friday night, he would knock on her door and hand her the flowers.

She would always feign surprise. "Why, Jonas, you shouldn't have. Now just where did you find such lovely flowers?" Then she would place one flower in a vase for Molly's room and arrange the others on her kitchen table.

For the Fourth of July, Sarah stocked watermelons, sweet corn, and cantaloupes. Jonas showed up that afternoon thumping on the watermelons to make sure they were ripe. He purchased five of them, along with ten cantaloupes and six dozen ears of sweet corn.

"Now, just how on earth are you going to eat all of that?" Sarah asked.

"I'm having a cookout. Oh, and by the way, you and Molly are invited of course. I want you to meet all of my family and some of my closest friends. I want them to know that I am dating the most beautiful girl in all of Mississippi."

Sarah blushed and turned away. She had been dating Jonas exclusively for almost three months. But for just a moment, she felt herself being swept away from him. And even though she was fighting to stay with him, something just didn't feel right.

"What's wrong, Sarah? Did I say the wrong thing? It's just… we've been dating since April and I would really like you to meet my mom and brothers. I know you'd like them. And my mother—she hasn't even met you and she already loves you!

"Sure, sure, we'll come. But now's not the place to be talking about our feelings. I have customers to take care of," she explained, just as a middle-aged couple scanned the hanging baskets on the display tables.

"Well, Sarah, it seems like there's never a good time to talk about feelings," he said, with hurt in his eyes. Without saying another word, Jonas turned and walked away.

That evening, as Sarah closed her shop, she wondered if Jonas would even pick her up for his party. But when she arrived at her house around five thirty that evening, with Molly in tow, he was waiting on her front porch.

"Ready for dinner and fireworks, ladies?" he asked.

"Sure. Just give Molly and me a minute to change. How can you have a party and just up and leave?" she asked him.

"Well, my mom is helping out long enough for me to pick up my two special guests," he said.

As they drove to Jonas's house, Sarah was deep in thought. Jonas discussed the fireworks display with Molly, assuring her there would be plenty of sparklers just for her. At the party, Jonas proudly introduced Sarah and Molly to his mother, two brothers and numerous friends. Sarah felt so special and welcomed. She kept a close eye on Molly and noticed how Jonas took the little girl's hand and showed her the fireworks clustered on a hilltop that extended beyond the back lawn. Sarah smiled as Molly shrieked in delight when she saw the assortment of bottle rockets, roman candles, and shooting stars that would soon light up the sky.

Around nine fifteen, as darkness enveloped the back yard, Jonas began setting off the fireworks. About halfway through the fireworks display, Jonas waved to his brother, Jake, to take over. As promised, Jonas brought Molly her sparklers and lit one for her. Molly waved her sparkler as if it were a magic wand.

Jonas looked for Sarah in the crowd and found her lounging in the swing on the back porch. He slid against her body and put his arm around her. Sarah could smell his cologne and the smoke from the fireworks and was drawn to his scent, his skin, his touch. He drew her face to his and kissed her passionately. Sarah cupped his face in her hands, exploring his jaw line, wanting to know every line, every crevice on his body.

"Wow, what fireworks tonight!" said Jonas.

"There just might be," whispered Sarah. She had resisted intimacy with him all summer. But tonight she felt safe in his arms.

The fireworks display was over shortly before ten o'clock, and the guests, including Jonas's family, hastily said their good-byes and left.

"I'll help you clean up before I leave," said Sarah.

"No, you don't have to do that. It'll give me something to do tomorrow. I'm sure you have to work tomorrow," said Jonas.

"I'm going in late tomorrow. I'm not opening up until ten. I insist on helping you. Molly's getting tired. If you don't mind, I'm going to make her lie down on your couch. She is so tired; she should be out cold in no time."

Sarah guided Molly to the living room couch, without a protest. She took a blanket and pillow from a closet and crafted a makeshift bed for her daughter. As Sarah recited a bedtime story about dancing horses, Molly drifted off to sleep.

Jonas entered the room and touched Sarah on the shoulder. His touch sparked inner desires she had restrained for too long.

"How am I going to take you home when Molly is out cold on my couch?" he asked, looking straight into her eyes. A strand of her blonde hair had fallen across her bright-blue eyes, and he gently pulled it back.

"I think it might be best if she slept here," said Sarah softly.

"Are you sure?" he asked.

"As sure as I've ever been about anything," she replied.

Jonas kissed her tenderly, taking her hand and guiding her to his open bedroom door. As though she were weightless, he picked up her willing body and carried her to the bed. He undressed her slowly, carefully, unbuttoning her white blouse and caressing her breasts. She unbuttoned his shirt, and then slid off her denim shorts before unzipping his pants, throwing them to the floor. Passionately, their bodies came together for the first time.

Sarah woke up early and reached for Jonas, but he was not there. She turned over to look for him. For a second, she panicked. Wayne left her one morning and never came back. But then she smelled coffee brewing and smiled. Jonas was not Wayne and would never be like him.

Jonas poured coffee and fixed breakfast for his two guests.

Sarah woke Molly, fed her breakfast, and hurriedly walked toward the door.

"I have to get going. I don't want to be late for work."

He turned her toward him. "If I had my way, you would never have to work, never want for anything," he whispered.

"But you have to understand, Jonas. I enjoy what I do," she explained.

"And you're good at it, too," he replied. "Whatever makes you happy, beautiful lady. See you two girls this evening? How about dinner?" he asked.

"Make it my place," Sarah replied.

Knowing she didn't have a baby-sitter for Molly that day, she drove straight to the shop. Two customers waited outside the rope she used to cordon off her shop when it was closed.

That day seemed to run smoothly, just like all the other days in Sunflower.

But one event was different. For weeks, Molly had admired a navy sailor dress from a window display in a shop downtown. Because Molly's sixth birthday was just two days away, Sarah planned to leave her shop long enough to buy the dress as a surprise birthday gift for her. With the profits from the weekend, she had enough money in her pocket to buy Molly's presents and to order a birthday cake from the nearby bakery. As she prepared a list for the party, Sarah knew she wanted Jonas at the celebration. Wanted him in her life forever. Molly had grown to love him and hadn't asked about her father for weeks.

Sarah swallowed hard before she asked Mr. Porter the only favor since she'd signed his lease agreement months ago. She asked him if he could have someone watch her shop for an hour while she bought her daughter's birthday presents.

"I'll see what I can do for you, Sarah. You have paid your rent on time," he replied. "I'll send someone over in about, say…thirty minutes?"

Sarah made a list of items to purchase for Molly's birthday as she quickly watered the plants and tidied up. About forty-five minutes later, Little Joe came to her shop.

"My dad sent me over here. Can you tell me—does everything here have a price tag?"

"Everything should be marked. Let me show you how the cash register works. It's so slow you may not even see a customer. And Molly—you won't even know she's here. She has a book to read. And many thanks," said Sarah.

"Not a problem," replied Little Joe.

Sarah was gone less than an hour, as she worried about Little Joe taking care of her customers. She carefully placed all of the packages under the back seat of the van, safe from her daughter's watchful eye.

When she returned to the shop, Little Joe was sitting on a chair in the middle of the aisles of plants.

"You were right, Sarah. Not a customer," he said.

Sarah looked around for Molly and didn't see her. She looked inside the shop and still didn't see her. Thinking she was in the bathroom, Sarah walked over to the open door and peered inside, but Molly wasn't there. Panic began to set in.

"Joe, where's Molly?" shrieked Sarah. Her heart sounded like a drum, beating high into her chest.

"Sarah, she was right here. She was reading inside the shop, and I didn't notice that she left. Beanie stopped by on his bike. But he was the only person I saw come by the shop. I'm sorry," replied Little Joe.

Sarah immediately closed the shop and sprinted through the streets, desperately searching for her daughter. Peering down each alleyway and back street, she screamed Molly's name. She inquired at each shop downtown, but no one in the local shops had seen her.

With each minute, the hope of finding her daughter lessened. She feared Molly had been kidnapped. But before she notified the police, Sarah decided to check the shop one last time, praying Molly had returned.

As she rounded the corner, she heard a child's wail, a scream she knew emanated from Molly. Seeing her little girl holding Big Joe's hand right by the entrance to the repair shop, she ran to her daughter's side. As she held Molly tightly to her chest, she noticed the torn dress and scratches on her arms.

"Molly, dear Molly. Mommy has been so worried about you. Are you OK?"

Molly adamantly shook her head no.

"Where have you been?"

"A bad man took me away. The man on the bike."

"Joe, did you hear that? It had to be Beanie. He's always gawked at Molly and me. He gives me the creeps."

Big Joe took in a big breath, pulling his glasses off in disbelief. "Now wait a minute, Sarah. Beanie has been right here with me all along. He's in the shop now. He couldn't have taken your little girl."

"Joe, where did you find my daughter?"

Joe appeared to ignore her and said nothing.

Sarah was visibly trembling. Beanie sat on a threadbare blue chair in the waiting room, his back to her. Anger welled inside her as she clenched her fists in rage.

"OK, I see how it is. I'm closing up shop right now. I've got to take care of my daughter. If my customers are looking for me, tell them I'm not feeling well. Got it?"

Sarah went home to get her thoughts together. Her daughter needed to see a doctor, but not in this town. She bathed her daughter, and her suspicions were confirmed, seeing dried blood in her panties.

"Mommy, it hurts real bad down there. The man with the beard. He took me for a ride on his bike. He promised to buy me a toy. But he did things that hurt me."

Fighting back tears, Sarah scrubbed Molly's body as if she could wash away the guilt and shame. But a pool of fear and despair surrounded them. And as the water left the tub and swirled down the open drain, the pain and suffering remained.

Sarah dried her daughter's tears and wiped her body dry with a fluffy towel. She lay down next to Molly in bed, trying to console her. Sarah's mind was racing. Suddenly, her next move was obvious.

Sarah packed what belongings she needed and left the rest in the cottage. She made out two envelopes, one to her landlady and one to Jonas. She had four months left on her lease and she paid that in full. The letter to Jonas was carefully crafted.

Dear Jonas,

Because of you, I had a wonderful spring and summer here in Sunflower. The best moments of my life were spent here with you and Molly. I will always remember how you made me feel safe and loved. Please keep that memory alive. But don't try to find me. I cannot stay here, and our relationship has to end. Your future is here in Sunflower, and mine is not.

You have been the love of my life, and I will never forget you.
Always,
Sarah

At seven the next morning, Sarah knew Jonas had already left for work, so she drove by his house and placed the letter in his mailbox. She wept silently, knowing how her sudden disappearance would hurt him.

Leaving Molly with the baby-sitter, Sarah decided to look for the one man who might know the true story. Daylight was just creeping through the town, but Sarah knew Tex would be starting his rounds five blocks from her flower shop and out of the watchful eye of Joe and Little Joe.

She let out a shrill whistle to get Tex's attention and motioned him over to her parked van. Tex crossed the street, and she opened the passenger door, motioning for him to get in.

"Tex, Beanie hurt my daughter yesterday. Do you know anything about that?"

Tex looked away, his eyes noticeably shifting behind his thick black glasses. "I can't say. I don't know anything."

Sarah made him look at her. "Tex, what do you know? I'm not gonna get you in trouble. Please, you have to tell me."

Tex looked at her and then turned away, speaking so low Sarah could barely hear him. "Beanie, he took your little girl for a ride on his bicycle. I think she wanted to go. He took her down the alleyway next to the bakery. He told me he had a toy for her. Told me to keep on the lookout 'cause it was a surprise. Gave me five dollars to make sure no one saw. I waited and watched for him until they came out. Then I left."

"Tex, that's what I needed to know."

Tex, in his innocence, looked at her lamely. "Did Beanie hurt your daughter, Miss Sarah?"

"Yes, he did bad things to her. But you didn't know, Tex."

"I'm real sorry, Miss Sarah. Could I get you a doughnut or a cup of coffee?"

"No thanks, Tex. I've got a few errands to run."

Sarah went to Joe's shop. It was early, but already Joe and Little Joe were busy moving cars to the work bays. She tapped Big Joe on the shoulder. "I need to speak with you *now!*"

Beanie was in the lobby, his bike parked next to her shop. She glared at him and took Joe aside.

"Sarah, I'm glad you're back. You've had four or five customers looking for you. I told them you'd be back soon."

"Your buddy over there, Beanie…he…he raped my daughter right under your eyes. You're covering for him."

"Sarah, he was sitting right there the whole time."

"That's not true. Little Joe says Beanie came by my shop while I was gone. You're lying. But I see what's going on. Tell you what. I'm gonna be closed today. I have to take care of my daughter. You know—I have to file a police report. There'll be a lot of police officers coming around asking you and Beanie questions."

Sarah angrily walked through the lobby, past the chair where Beanie sat nervously stroking his white beard. She stopped right in front of him.

"I promise you, Beanie. You'll pay for what you did to my daughter. I'll see to that."

Beanie didn't even have a chance to respond. Sarah kicked over his bike perched next to her shop. Methodically, she watered her plants for one last time and left her rope and "closed" sign in plain view. She then picked up Molly from the baby-sitter, leaving Sunflower behind for good.

No one ever heard from her again. So when Beanie turned up dead in the same alleyway where Tex said Beanie had taken Molly, Sarah became a person of interest in the crime. It was Little Joe who found Beanie face down in a pool of his own blood, a knife plunged deep in his back.

Everyone who knew Sarah and Beanie were questioned. Joe and Little Joe were the first two the police interrogated. They even questioned Tex. It was noted that Tex had scratches and bruises on his upper arms. Tex said he fell on the concrete while he was delivering breakfast to the ladies at the bank. Knowing how clumsy Tex was, the police removed him from the list of suspects.

———

Five years have passed since Beanie's murder. To this day, Sarah is still the main suspect in Beanie's death. Police are still hoping to bring her in for questioning. But she seems to have vanished into thin air. Even Jonas never heard from her.

Like many days during the summer, people in the town stop and linger at the dilapidated corner. Some whisper about Sarah and how she is still a murder suspect in Beanie's death. Tex still pauses to think about Sarah and what happened to Beanie. Mr. Cartwright drops by and sometimes leaves flower petals, remembering Sarah's kindness to him…how Mrs. Cartwright would have loved her! And the old twins stop by even though they never purchased one item from the shop. They remember how concerned Sarah always was about them and how she had once given them an envelope with twenty dollars enclosed so their electricity wouldn't be cut off.

On this particular day in July—the fifth anniversary of her disappearance—Jonas is seen placing a beautiful bouquet of pink roses and baby's breath on an empty wooden pallet, where Sarah had displayed her plants years before. But this is the last day the townspeople will see flowers left where Sarah had once assisted customers with her beautiful arrangements and friendly service. Jonas is ready to move on with his life.

On this July 6th, Jonas has waited long enough. He happens to remember Sarah hails from Pittsburgh and has family in Atlanta. Just yesterday, he hired a private detective to locate her mother and in turn, find Sarah. He had been lonely too long, and decided to pursue every avenue to find her.

As Jonas drives away from his hometown, the only place he's ever lived, he thinks about new roads, new adventures that stretch out in front of him. He had a comfortable life in Sunflower, but it didn't mean anything without having Sarah with him to enjoy it.

Driving north on Route 3, past the small towns of Pentecost and Blaine, he likes his odds of finding Sarah. She once told him soul mates always find a way of coming together when they least expect it. Fate always steps in. He smiles down at a single rose he took with him, the rose for tomorrow. Two roses, the one for yesterday and today, he left in the center of Sunflower, atop the unkempt grass where he first met Sarah years ago. The flower girl, like the strongest magnet, was pulling him toward her.

GREEN APPLE GIRL

I remember leaving the warmth of a wood-burning kitchen hearth in early spring for the chilly outdoors. From the back porch, I would jump down the five narrow steps and hit the ground running. Gingerly, I would slide under the familiar boards of a faded brown fence that served as the boundary between my family's property and our closest neighbor. Weaving my way cautiously through tall dead grass, I would wander until I reached a path to a white frame house with bright green shutters. I'd rap on the door, and a thin old woman with long white hair and sparkling hazel eyes would greet me with a cheery "Hello my Green Apple Girl. Come on in." Every welcome was the same, but somehow each visit was special and different.

"Aunt Frances," as I endearingly called her, would always invite me to sit at her kitchen table while she fixed me some sort of treat. Even though she'd keep her eye on me constantly as she peered into her kitchen pantry (as if she were afraid I would rob her of some precious jewels), I loved every minute of our visits. Sometimes for a special treat, she'd serve lime-green Jell-O with pineapple and carrots, or cherry Jell-O with fruit cocktail. Other times she'd brew tea in an exotic teapot and use her best china cups.

But the best part of my visits was meeting her newest pets. Cats lounged lazily on scatter rugs. A Dalmatian and a black Labrador retriever ruled the back yard for a decade or more. A baby squirrel she had nursed back to health nested safely in a wire cage. She even had a "teacup dog," which she carried in the palm of her hand and gingerly petted.

I'd sit at her kitchen table and dream of my future as she talked about her past. She spoke about her days working in big cities and living in small apartments while I envisioned seeing those sights myself. Being the youngest of five children and living in a rural area made me hungry for a life I had never experienced.

Sometimes she'd talk about how she came back home to care for her ailing mother and father. I'd sit with rapt attention as she talked about caring for them until the day they died. My mother often told me Aunt Frances gave up marriage and a family to care for her parents.

Summers were the most memorable visits with Aunt Frances. As soon as my chores were done, I'd follow the familiar, narrow path through unsightly grass. Aunt Frances only mowed a thin strip of grass in her yard for her pets. She told me that mowing grass hurt the wild animals, the birds, squirrels, and rabbits. Her house looked forbidden and unwelcoming on the outside. A big "No Trespassing" sign was posted in her driveway. Other kids told me she was crazy and to stay away from her. But the warnings made me want to visit her all the more. In fact, I was probably one of the few people she welcomed into her house.

Late June marked frequent trips to the swimming hole for my brothers and me. We had a well-worn trail through the tall grass across Aunt Frances's property. One day, we were taking that shortcut when we saw Aunt Frances wearing gumboots, blue jeans, and a long-sleeved shirt. In her right hand she toted a shotgun. My brothers started laughing and took off running.

"Who wears gum boots and blue jeans when it's this hot out? And why does she have a gun?" asked my oldest brother, laughing out loud.

"That old lady is nuts," my other brother remarked.

Shamefully, I remained silent while my brothers mocked my dear friend.

My next visit with Aunt Frances was the following day.

"Was that you I saw with your brothers going across my property?" she asked me.

"Yes, ma'am," I said, and held my breath, thinking she was going to be angry with us for trespassing.

"Well, just be careful," she said. "The snakes are out now. That's why I wear my boots and jeans and carry my shotgun. You just never know when you'll step on one. If I see one, I'm going to blow its head off."

Her paranoia with snakes continued, and every summer she could be seen in heavy boots and long-sleeved clothing, stepping precariously to her mailbox.

Late June or the first of July would mark the ripening of the "June" or Lodi apples. Because her property wrapped around our front yard, I would often take a shortcut up a steep hill and walk under the heavy branches of one of her apple trees. I loved to eat those green apples and was known to eat so many that my stomach rumbled in agony. Many early summer days I arrived at her house with a green apple in my hand, munching on its tart juicy flesh. Aunt Frances would laugh and say she didn't know how I could stand to eat those sour things. During one of those visits, voraciously eating green apples, she nicknamed me her Green Apple Girl.

Aunt Frances loved the old-fashioned apple trees so much; she planted two more in her front yard. Every year when the fruit ripened, she'd invite me to her front porch. As I'd pick ripe apples, she'd sit on her front porch chatting incessantly. On those visits, she'd give me big paper bags and invited me to fill them.

"Tell your mom to fry these up for supper," she'd say. "These apples fry up nicely."

Her front porch had four massive columns and a set of thick concrete stairs, stirring my childhood imagination to think of her house as a Southern mansion. In the center of the porch was a chandelier that draped down, decorated with brass trim. As I sat on the front porch one hot July day, eating green apples, I imagined myself all grown up in a pink gossamer gown, dancing under the stars with handsome young men.

As I approached my teen years, visits with Aunt Frances became less frequent. Her habit of not wanting to turn her back on me, or leave me alone in the house, was more apparent. My feelings were hurt because I felt she couldn't trust me. My mother said her mistrust came from living in big cities alone and fearful.

When I'd make those infrequent visits, she'd still prepare treats and bestow me with small gifts—an old doll or one of her childhood toys. On one special visit, she made me a cup of tea and began to talk in a low voice about a man she had deeply loved. She didn't give his name, but told me he asked her to marry him.

"I would have married him too, but that's when my mother got sick. I did what was expected of me. I came home and took care of her and my father," she whispered, as a tear rolled down her cheek.

It was hard for me to imagine her young and in love. Gray now peppered her hair, and deep wrinkles creased her slender face. But although her back stooped with age, she still managed to have a twinkle in her hazel eyes.

"I'm glad I have you, my green apple girl. If anything happens to me, I want you to have first chance at buying this place," Aunt Frances said.

I looked up at her in astonishment. I was all of twelve years old.

"Aunt Frances, I do love this house. I sometimes dream about this house. My promise to you is that I will take care of it. But I don't want to talk about anything happening to you," I responded.

She changed the subject and brought out some packaged sugar cookies, while promising me she'd make Jell-O in honor of my next visit.

The next year, I started high school and was very busy with sports, schoolwork, and friends. Although I had good intentions, I didn't visit my friend very often. Years passed, and I went to college out of state and got married. During that hectic time in my life, I rarely communicated with Aunt Frances.

One day, my mother called to convey sad news; Aunt Frances had fallen ill and was living in town with a niece, her closest relative. On my next visit home, my mother and I walked across Aunt Frances's property. The place looked deserted. Dense, tall weeds surrounded her house, partially hiding the green shutters. A house so grand in my memory was now covered in blistered, peeling paint.

"It's such a shame, as pretty as this place used to be," my mother commented.

On occasion, I visited Aunt Frances while she was living with her niece, but it was never quite the same. Now Aunt Frances's fingers were gnarled with arthritis. Weak and feeble, she slowly arose from bed utilizing a walker. But she still remembered how I loved her green apples. Although she hadn't seen me for years, we chatted as if our long-ago visits occurred yesterday. I silently wondered if she remembered our talk years ago about me purchasing her house, but I didn't feel comfortable bringing up the subject. I felt if she truly wanted me to buy her house, she'd offer it to me.

As more years passed, I spent my time raising three children and working full time. I lost touch with Aunt Frances. Occasionally, I would think about my childhood visits with her and especially those infrequent visits on the front porch. From time to time, I would recollect childhood dreams of one day owning the house.

About ten years after my last visit with her, I heard she had passed away. Her funeral was a very private affair with only a few family members in attendance. Distant relatives, the only family she had, inherited her house and its contents. I learned the house would be sold at public auction, then later received word it had already been sold.

A few years later, I received a phone call. A woman with a friendly voice quickly introduced herself as Eileen Shultz and announced she was the owner of Aunt Frances's property. While going through Aunt Frances's personal belongings left in the house, she found a small box with my name on the back of it.

"Feel free to drop by at your convenience to receive your part of her estate," Eileen urged.

A few weeks later, I accepted her invitation. As I approached the house, I noticed a yard neatly mowed. Distant memories resurfaced of those childhood visits, drinking tea and eating Jell-O, while hearing stories of living in small apartments in big cities. Memories of sharing cookies with squirrels and having tea in one cup and a teacup dog in another flooded my being.

But somehow the house seemed so much smaller than my recollections. I asked to go to the front porch one last time, and Eileen, a plump middle-aged woman, graciously escorted me up the steep porch steps. However, my favorite memory of the house seemed less grand than what I remembered. A once-elaborate chandelier was now rusted and swayed precariously in the slight breeze. Even the cherished apple trees in the front yard brandished decay and dead branches.

I was invited upstairs and Eileen showed me Aunt Frances's picture albums. I found myself staring at a picture of a young Aunt Frances, in Tahiti, wearing a two-piece bathing suit. On a beautiful tropical beach, long dark hair framing her glowing face, Aunt Frances perched atop the broad shoulders of a handsome young man. Pictures of other boy-friends during exotic island vacations appeared on postcards. So this was Aunt Frances, before she grew old and humpbacked. A story unfolded of an attractive young woman leading a glamorous life…the life she let me glimpse in her stories when I was a child. Her other life stretched in front of me, adventurous possibilities she sacrificed to care for her parents and a menagerie of animals.

"Thank you for sharing this with me," I said and swallowed hard. "Some of my favorite childhood memories were spent in this house with her."

"Well, you must have been very special to her. She left you this." Eileen handed me a cardboard box wrapped in faded tissue paper. Although filled with curiosity to know the contents of the package, I didn't open it then. Gingerly, I clutched the small box tightly in my hand as I left the familiar house for the last time.

"Thanks Eileen," I said. "I'm glad you got this house. And I'm so happy that you've taken care of all of her things."

Eileen laughed. "It's like I know her, through her pictures and her personal belongings. But you must have meant a lot to her. Frances specifically left you this box."

And as quickly as our visit began, I said good-bye to the lady who had bought what I thought I always wanted.

I didn't open the box until I was alone in my bedroom. This seemed like a momentous occasion, and I held my breath as I began to open the mysterious box. Sure enough, on the bottom of the box was my name, in Aunt Frances's best handwriting. Nestled inside faded newspaper were two miniature, framed Hummel prints. Each petite picture displayed an elf-like little girl perched on the branch of an apple tree, a green apple clenched in her hand.

These quaint prints still adorn my bedroom wall...treasured gifts that remind me of childhood hopes and dreams—dreams initiated long ago on Aunt Frances's columned front porch. Although all grown up, part of me remains the Green Apple Girl.

DREAM HOUSE

She walked up the three porch steps for the last time on a hot summer day. It was just after two o'clock, and she gingerly avoided the second step that was sagging and about to give way under her weight. As she entered the house (now devoid of furniture and pictures on the walls) she noticed how much smaller the house seemed. In the middle of the kitchen floor were the last of the boxes of family belongings. Spice racks and old pots and pans shared space in plastic bags with picture albums, soccer balls, and basketball trophies.

This was the day she'd anticipated for years. Finally, the dream house (a five year project) was completed. Through the woods past this little gray cottage stood the impressive columned structure. To the new house she'd take the last of the boxes and close the door to the cottage forever. She paused to look past the dishwasher that hadn't worked for two years, past the smudges of children's fingerprints on painted walls. The kitchen floor was covered in dark-green linoleum that was cracked and faded. The floor had withstood the incessant pounding of children dribbling basketballs hour after hour. The faded walls once housed the sports fantasies of children playing starring roles for future basketball teams, dreams that became a reality from workouts years ago in that crowded kitchen.

As her mind filled with nostalgia, she walked across the kitchen to look at the penciled lines on wood trim next to the landing that led into a narrow hallway. All four children had proudly etched their names next to their height markings and dates in pencil. How she wanted to rip the board from the wall and take it with her.

From the kitchen, she descended the steps to the bedrooms down a narrow hallway and quietly entered her oldest son's bedroom. On the walls, his artistic hands had drawn the perfect shot for basketball and had penciled in all the phone numbers of his high school basketball team, and his basketball goals for the future. She remembered how she would cringe when company came, thinking that most mothers would have rightfully yelled and screamed about drawings and writings on the wall. But then she thought to herself about her son becoming a standout college basketball player and softly closed the door.

She paused in her daughter's room, adjacent to her own. These walls, once filled with a little girl's laughter, were now empty except for black trash bags filled with outgrown clothes and broken toys. Next to the bags was a crumpled poster featuring a young athletic woman lifting a barbell over her head with the caption "Strength." She never imagined she'd need "strength" to say good-bye to all these memories.

Remembering all the times she tucked her daughter in bed at night, read her stories or wiped away her tears, she found it difficult to leave the tiny alcove that just last month seemed so dreadful. Never again would she walk into that room to kiss her daughter goodnight.

Next to her daughter's room, she entered her own bedroom for one last time. She briefly stared at the cracks in the ceiling before her eyes glanced toward the now empty space that used to be her closet. Embarrassed by how chipped and faded the folded doors appeared in the bright sunlight, she wondered how she ever stuffed all of her clothes into that tiny closet. The corner next to the window looked lost without her computer desk. She closed her eyes and saw herself staying up late at night, working feverishly on all those research papers for her master's degree.

She remembered trying to fall asleep on hot summer nights, desperately wondering if she'd be in that tiny crowded house for the rest of her life. Then she thought about all of the Christmas presents she'd wrapped for her children in that room, the door bolted so they wouldn't see.

Retracing her steps, she entered each room for one last time. Memories flooded her mind as if she were paging through a photo album year by year of the time spent in this house. She paused for one last time at the space where the kitchen table used to be and thought about all of the meals shared in that space with her family. On Saturday afternoons, she prepared double chocolate chip cookies her children devoured. Every Sunday at breakfast, each family member had to give every family member a compliment. Sometimes humorous, but always kind, she laughed out loud as she remembered her best compliments from her husband and children. Her oldest son jokingly called her the Family Enforcer, while her husband once romantically affirmed he loved her more with each passing day.

She exited the front door and locked it firmly, with tears in her eyes. She regretted all the nights she was in a bad mood, yearning for a new house, wanting her space, feeling she had sacrificed career goals to keep her family strong. As she walked down the faded deck one last time, she realized perhaps the best moments of her life were spent in this little crowded house with cracks in the floor and a crooked set of steps that led upstairs. As she walked down the faded deck to the narrow front yard overlooking the highway, an old soccer ball reminded her of competitive family games on the front lawn. In the back yard, an old basketball hoop, (used so often for one-on-one family rivalries) was silenced forever.

She was suddenly overcome with sadness, a feeling of leaving a time and space where she could never return. After so many years of wanting to leave, she was shocked by her emotions. She bit her lower lip to fight back the tears, then suddenly stopped, frozen in her tracks, in the hot summer sun. She ran across the yard, bolted up the front stairs, and unlocked the front door. Grabbing a claw hammer from a toolbox amid the kitchen boxes, she ripped the board from the kitchen wall... the board with the pencil marks of her children's heights and names and dates long gone. Some traditions cannot be forgotten.

This time, she closed the door for good and walked back to her new house, the house she'd dreamed of building since she was a child. As she approached the front porch of her new home, she clutched the treasured board to her chest. Regardless of décor, she will hang this board, her memory tree, in her new kitchen. Dream homes are wherever dreams are kept alive.

EXTRAORDINARY KINDNESS

Sometimes ordinary people get to do extraordinary things. Some gesture or act of kindness may touch another's life briefly. Generosity from someone you hardly know can change your destiny. For me, that person was Dr. Catherine Tice.

Dr. Tice was a tiny wisp of a lady with a reputation for being cold and pragmatic. Silver hair framed her thin face and sharp nose. Prim and proper, she carried herself with the dignity that earned her the title Dean of Science. I was never sure of her age, but she appeared to be in her mid-sixties. She was cordial, polite, and always professional, yet viewed by many students as aloof and intimidating.

I met Dr. Tice for the first time in 1996, when I returned to school to pursue a teaching degree. Occasionally, I would meet with her, to have necessary paperwork signed for routine matters such as dropping or adding a class. Except for polite exchanges, our conversations were minimal.

In December 1997, I had one semester left before graduation. At the matronly age of forty, I was an atypical student. Yet I was eagerly determined to achieve and excel. Maintaining a straight A average while raising four small children and working part time was a source of personal pride. However, a roadblock loomed ahead I had not anticipated.

Sharpsburg University was a small private Methodist college only ten miles from my home. Unfortunately, tuition was very expensive. Due to a serious illness, our family had incurred a huge debt, and our credit was tarnished. Because of our poor credit, I was only eligible to borrow a small portion of my tuition costs.

In January of 1998, I received a bill for my final year at Sharpsburg. After my loan proceeds, I still owed the university $5,800. Of that amount, I had only eight hundred and five dollars. It was two days before classes would commence, so I contemplated my next course of action. I decided to speak with someone in the business office, level with him or her, and work out a payment plan. In the past, the business office worked with me, and I had always made payment arrangements on time.

As I waited in line with my current bill, I silently rehearsed what I would say to the cashier. When it was my turn, a young lady with long brown hair and a round face greeted me listlessly with a faint smile.

"Your balance, miss, is fifty-eight hundred dollars," she stated.

"Yes, but I would like to work out a payment arrangement with your business manager. I can only pay eight hundred dollars today. So I would like to discuss a payment plan to pay the remaining five thousand," I said in a hushed tone. It was embarrassing for me to have everyone in the lobby hear about my financial predicament.

"I'm sorry, but we cannot help you. Part of the money you owe is from last semester. You must pay the amount in full before five tomorrow, or your classes will be dropped automatically," she snapped.

"I would like to see the office manager. She has always worked with me in the past," I insisted.

"We have a policy in place-- we do not make payment plans for the last semester of a student's senior year," she retorted.

"But I have made payment arrangements in the past. And you can check my academic record here at the university. I have always made my extended payments on schedule. Please check with the manager." I was trembling inside, trying to maintain composure.

Obviously this lady with her rules and nasty demeanor did not know my many late nights cramming for finals or the financial sacrifices I had made to be here. I was *not* going to let her stand in my way of graduating on time.

"One moment, please," the young lady said and disappeared inside the business manager's office.

After a few minutes, but what seemed to be an eternity, she returned. My dilemma had caused a huge line of students behind me, and it was apparent the cashier was perturbed at the inconvenience.

"Miss, we cannot make extended payments for your last semester. This is the university's policy, and the business manager just confirmed that. Can't you borrow the money from someone?" she asked.

I was not about to tell this lady the awful truth. Because of a serious illness not covered by medical insurance, my family was on the verge of bankruptcy. My husband and I had agreed we would pay everyone back; bankruptcy was not an option. So month-by-month, we were paying every creditor back, every last cent.

"Ma'am, I really don't understand the problem. If I don't pay the money, you can simply withhold my diploma. I need to graduate this spring so I can get a job teaching this fall. I need your help," I pleaded with this unyielding woman.

"You and about two thousand other students," she replied callously and pushed me aside. "May I help the next person in line?"

Dejected, I left the business office and walked randomly around the small campus. The air was cold and a bitter wind was blowing, but I was oblivious to the elements. In a daze, I walked to the library and sat at a table next to the magazine racks. I stared at a newspaper lying on the table, but couldn't focus on the words.

Suddenly, I realized I could not lose my composure. But I *had* to do something. At home, four children were depending on me to finish school and get a teaching job. I could drop out for one semester to work full time and complete my course work in the fall. But that plan would set me back one complete year. Teachers were hired in the spring for the upcoming school year. By not graduating on time, I would lose an entire year's salary.

After contemplating several options, I remembered Dr. Tice. I would make an appointment to see her. She could vouch for my grades and my academic record. If she could write a letter or make a phone call on my behalf, then maybe the business office wouldn't drop my classes.

My heart pounding, I walked the short distance from the library to Dean Tice's office.

"May I help you?" Dr. Tice's secretary asked.

"I need an appointment to see Dr. Tice, at her earliest convenience."

"Dr. Tice is in meetings all day today," she responded.

"It is a matter of utmost urgency," I pleaded. "I have to see her before classes begin."

"She can see you tomorrow at eleven, for just a short time," the secretary suggested.

"It won't take long. Thank you. I'll be here at eleven," I replied.

The next morning, I arrived fifteen minutes early. My future depended on this meeting. If it did not go well, my classes would be dropped at five that day for nonpayment. And if this occurred, my career would be placed on hold indefinitely.

At precisely eleven o'clock, Dr. Tice opened her door and escorted me inside, leaving the door slightly ajar.

"Jessica, how are you today?" she asked politely.

Just fine, Dr. Tice. But I need your advice on a matter." I tried to appear calm, even though I was trembling inside.

She looked at me with concern.

"Dr. Tice, I'm not sure if you know this, but I have worked very hard since I've been here, and I have a straight A average. I am on track to graduate this spring."

"Yes, I'm quite aware of your academic excellence. We here at Sharpsburg are proud of your accomplishments," she responded.

"Well, I may not be graduating on time. You see, I have four children at home, and I don't have the money to pay for this semester." I paused, tears rolling down my cheeks.

Dr. Tice reached for a box of tissues on her desk. Her aged hand extended the box to me. As I reached for it, her hand gripped mine.

"Now, dear, get your composure."

I continued, sniffling into my crumpled tissue as I spoke. "I have tried to work with financial aid, but they have refused." Again, tears filled my eyes uncontrollably. "I have offered them a payment plan, but they told me that is not possible because it's my last semester. If I do not pay them in full by the end of the business day today, my classes will be dropped."

"They told you that?" she asked in disbelief.

"Yes, and when I asked for help, the lady told me no, that me and two thousand other students needed help. So I thought maybe you could—"

Before I could finish my sentence, Dr. Tice rose from a massive cherry desk, her tiny silhouette a stark contrast to the large room. She peeped outside her door to make sure no one was within earshot and then shut the door softly. Returning to her desk, she opened the top drawer and took out her checkbook.

"Jessica, *no one*, absolutely *no one* at this university must know about this. Do you understand?" Dr. Tice's tone was sharp and controlling. "How much do you need?"

As I watched, Dr. Tice began writing a check to the university. Slowly, I began to realize the risk Dr. Tice was taking to help me.

"No, Dr. Tice, I can't accept a handout from you. I didn't come here for charity. I just came here for a letter of recommendation from you. If you would just write a letter for me to the business office—"

"I am embarrassed by how you were treated today. That should have never happened. How much do you need?" she persisted.

At first I couldn't find the words to answer her. I was deeply moved by her generosity.

"Dr. Tice, I owe the university five thousand dollars. But I could never ask you for that kind of money. You don't even know me, other than by my academic record. But thank you for your concern," I replied.

If Dr. Tice was shocked by the amount of money I owed the university, she didn't show it.

"This is not a handout. And you will pay me back. Believe me, I'll see to that." She eyed me intently and continued to write the check.

"Dr. Tice, the only way I can accept this check is if I write you an IOU, something formal," I responded through my tears.

"Fine, go ahead and drop that by my office if you like. But take this check to the business office today," she insisted. Dr. Tice's blue eyes were piercing right through me.

"Jessica, I know you are going to go out into the teaching world and do great things. All I ask is that you pay me back when you can. But again, absolutely *no* one can know at this university. It has to be our secret," she pleaded.

"Dr. Tice, I promise. And don't worry, I'll work hard to pay the money back as soon as I get my first paycheck, if not before."

"Dear, I don't doubt that at all," she responded, with a smile.

I ran straight from her office, up the hill to the business office. Ironically, it was the same woman who had waited on me yesterday, the one who had tried to slam the door on my future. She greeted me with the same plastic smile.

"I have this check to pay my account in full," I offered, grinning broadly.

The woman looked at the check. She gazed at the signature carefully and then stared at me, as if in disbelief. Then she stamped my account as paid in full.

I only saw Dr. Tice a few times that semester. Twice I met with her privately to make payments on the loan. Each time, she dismissed me brusquely, as if to deny the transaction had ever transpired.

In May I graduated summa cum laude. Dr. Tice inspired me to continue my quest to excel. On graduation day, my eyes were on her as she marched in with her fellow colleagues. After the ceremony, I looked for her to shake her hand and to thank her once more, but our paths never crossed.

That fall, I began my teaching career. With my first interview, I landed a teaching job. Keeping my pledge to Dr. Tice, each month I mailed a payment to her home address. Because she wanted to maintain the secrecy of the loan, she requested I mail all correspondence connected with the loan to her residence. After two years of monthly payments, I paid the debt in full. With the last payment, I enclosed a letter to her.

Dear Dr. Tice:

A few years ago, you barely knew me. And yet you bestowed upon me the greatest gift I have ever received. Your loan was based on a sense of trust in me, even though I was practically a total stranger. I will be forever in your debt.

Thanks to you I have become a teacher, and I am convinced that I do make a difference in my students' lives. Had it not been for your kindness, my career would have been delayed and may not have ever happened.

Enclosed is the last payment on my loan. Since that day in your office, when you handed me that check, I have been on a mission to make you proud. Every day I go to work, I think about your generosity. My only hope is that someday I will get the opportunity to help some person in need in much the same way you helped me. I will never forget you.

Sincerely,
Jessica Dawson

After graduation, I never saw Dr. Tice again. A few years ago, I heard she was somewhere in the Middle East, breaking tradition and educating young women utilizing Western philosophy, a potentially dangerous undertaking for an American. Yet this mission epitomizes the Dr. Tice I came to know on that January day in 1998. She was never afraid to take risks when championing women who show promise.

Since entering the teaching profession in the fall of 1998, I strive each day to be a good teacher and coach, wanting to make a positive impact on my students. Someway, somehow, I hope Dr. Tice knows of my aspiration to live up to her expectations. With one huge debit from her personal checkbook, she made it all possible.

Years later, I await the chance to perform an uplifting intervention, as Dr. Tice did for me. If the opportunity arises, I hope to demonstrate her generosity and courage. To write a five-thousand-dollar check, with no strings attached, to a total stranger might be labeled as crazy. But from my view, it is an ordinary person performing an extraordinary life-changing act of kindness.

555 SEMINAR DRIVE

It is seven o'clock, and Rita is finishing dinner. Chad is running late again. She cuts the oven off and turns the kitchen burners on low. Concerned about her appearance, she shuffles to the bedroom and stands in front of a gilded mirror, smoothing her print dress with trembling fingers. Turning her silhouette from side to side, she feigns a smile. As if in pain, she winces as she reflects on ghosts from the past. Instead of weary lines on her face, she sees a young beautiful woman, the woman she was thirty years ago. Suddenly, instead of viewing her countenance, she screams as the mirror erupts into shards of glass, slicing the image of who she was into an explosion of bloody flesh, leading into a black abyss.

———

Twenty years previously...

It was nine o'clock and dinner had been on the stove for over an hour. Rita grew tired of waiting and cut the stove off. The roast beef was dry, and the mashed potatoes were crusted over. She looked at the peas floating in butter and started to cry. One more dinner ruined.

Tonight at seven o'clock, he called. He was working overtime, but he called and said he'd definitely be home by eight. At eight o'clock, she lit the candle and dimmed the lights, so sure he'd be there any minute. But by eight thirty, melted wax dripped onto the oak table, so she blew out the candle and threw it in the trash.

Returning to the mirror, she needed reassurance about her appearance. She knew men thought her attractive. When she walked down the street, she held her head high and didn't look at them, but she could feel men's eyes on her. She brushed her long black hair and reapplied her lipstick. The traces of tears were gone.

At nine thirty, Chad came in the side door, a sheepish grin on his face. He smelled of grease and diesel fuel, his fingernails blackened from changing the oil in his pickup truck.

"I'm sorry, Rita. I tried to get here earlier, but Mike didn't show up for work today. And you know how my Dad is. We had to ship today or we'd be behind schedule."

Rita wiped the tears away and took the roast out of the oven. "You promised me you'd be home on time tonight. You also promised we'd go out dancing. You know how I love to dance." She closed her eyes and saw her body twirling across a wooden dance floor, strobe lights flashing overhead.

Chad was quiet, his soft eyes watching her as she placed their dinner on the table. He didn't say a word as he went to the sink and washed the grease from his hands. With his hands still dripping wet, he sat down next to her.

As they ate their meal in silence, Rita thought he hadn't even noticed the damask tablecloth and the good china for what was to be a romantic dinner before going out on the town.

After Chad finished eating, he took a shower while Rita washed the dishes. She knew Chad was too tired to take her anywhere. She felt a wave of loneliness overcome her. She had no friends to call, nowhere to go on a Saturday night. She was twenty-three, going on fifty.

Rita heard the splash from the shower and imagined Chad's taut body covered in soapy lather. She imagined him drying his body with a thick towel and then applying cologne after he shaved his angular face. She dreamed he changed into a light-blue knit shirt, the one she'd bought him last week. It showed off his brown eyes and boyish good looks. Then he slid into gabardine black pants and grabbed her hand tightly as they went toward the door, off for a much-needed romantic night on the town.

But in reality, Chad took a long hot shower and stumbled toward the bedroom. Wearily, he lay in bed and closed his eyes. Rita glanced through the open bedroom door and knew another night's plans were wasted. Through teary eyes, she slid off her aquamarine dress that showed every voluptuous curve. Clad only in her strapless bra and bikini underwear, she searched her closet for her white terrycloth robe. When she found it under a stack of never worn pajamas, she slammed the bedroom door behind her and strode barefoot into their tiny living room. She turned on their portable television set and switched aimlessly through the channels.

An hour later, she went to bed, lying by her husband. But as she closed her eyes, her mind was miles away. On a dance floor, she was gliding effortlessly with a handsome man. But when she looked into his eyes, he was not her husband. She shivered at even thinking these thoughts. Chad was a good, hardworking man. How could she think of being in the arms of anyone else?

———

The next day, Rita awakened before Chad. It was half past seven, and she knew Chad would sleep until at least ten o'clock. Chad worked seven days a week, but Sunday he rarely went to work before noon.

Rita put on a pair of running shorts, a T-shirt, and running shoes for her usual Sunday jog through the quiet neighborhood. Although the morning dew had not yet dried, the air was already heavy and humid, a typical summer morning in Charleston. As she jogged along, she heard a car behind her. Glancing over her shoulder, she saw a young man with long, dark hair driving a beat up Chevy appearing to follow her. She motioned for him to pass, but he stayed right behind her.

Frightened, she turned back toward her house and picked up the pace. She usually jogged three to five miles. But right now, all she wanted was to be safe with Chad at home. The young man pulled his dilapidated car beside her, rolled down his window and started yelling.

"Hey, baby, slow it down. Why don't you hop in my car? It's too hot to be runnin. I've got some other exercise in mind," he jeered.

Rita knew she had to think fast. "Buddy, no thanks. I'm already home. My big, strong police officer husband is waiting inside." Rita jogged into a yard in front of a yellow frame house, and as she reached the bottom step of the front porch, the young man sped off, screeching his wheels in haste.

Sweat was trickling down Rita's back and she realized how thirsty she was. As she slowly walked away from the house, a man came to the front door.

"Can I help you, miss?" he asked in a deep Southern drawl.

Rita turned around to see a muscular, attractive man with curly brown hair and ruddy complexion who looked to be in his late twenties.

"No thanks. I was out for my morning jog and a man was following me, making lewd comments. So I told him this was my house and my husband was a police officer. He floored the gas pedal and disappeared after that." As she spoke, she felt embarrassed by her appearance, her hair and body dripping with sweat.

"You look scared to death. Come on in and sit down and have a glass of ice water. Since you told him I'm a cop, the least I can do is to write up a police report," he joked.

Rita took a step closer to the large front porch. "No, no thanks. I can't come in looking like this. Besides, your wife may not like a strange woman in her house."

You don't have to worry about that. I don't have a wife. I've come close a few times, but old Shep here seems to scare them off," he said, pointing to his German shepherd lying on the porch.

Rita bent down to pet the dog, sprawled on his side. "He looks harmless to me," she said, and grinned.

"Believe me, Shep can spot a phony or a thug when they enter our yard. The last girlfriend I had, he growled every time she came near. He even tried to nudge in between us on the couch. I should have listened to him a long time ago about her," he said and then changed the subject.

"Come on in. If Shep hasn't torn your head off yet, that's a sign he likes you." Patrick couldn't help but notice her curvaceous body and was secretly hoping she'd take him up on his offer and come inside for a visit.

Rita smiled nervously. "I'll take you up on your offer for a glass of water. But let's just talk on the porch. I don't even know your name. For all I know, you could be an accomplice to that man who tried to pick me up."

"Do you think I look like that kind of man, miss?" he asked, disgusted by her comment. "Wait right here." He disappeared inside the house. Rita fiddled nervously with her hair. She had meant her comment as a joke. Silently, she wished she were already home safe instead of on a strange man's porch.

Pat returned a few minutes later with a pitcher of ice water. As he poured water into two crystal glasses she sucked in a deep breath. "Sorry, guess it was my idea of a joke. I was just trying to ask your name before we continued our conversation."

Pat waved off her apology. "No it's my fault. Really. I shouldn't have been offended by your comment. Guess I should socialize a little bit more. Ole Shep just wags his tail and pants whenever I talk to him. My name's Patrick Kelly. But call me Pat. What's yours?"

"Nice to meet you, Pat. I'm Rita. Rita Everitt.

"Rita. That's a pretty name. Is it a family name?" he asked.

"No, not a family name. I was named Rita because my dad loved margaritas so much. When he'd get half tipsy, he'd just order another round of 'ritas. So when I was born, he named me after his biggest vice," Rita confessed, and then changed the subject. "Patrick Kelly. Good Irish name."

"Yes, I'm afraid so. My mother still calls every weekend to make sure I've gone to confession. I must not be a good Catholic boy because even if I haven't, I lie to her. Then I have to go to confession for the lies," Patrick said with a chuckle.

"Well, Patrick, guess I should get going. But thanks for the water." Now Rita found herself not wanting to leave. She wanted to know more about Patrick Kelly.

"Sure you don't want to stay for breakfast? I can whip up some hotcakes in no time."

"Thanks anyway. I need to finish my run before I eat," she replied.

"Speaking of eating…how about dinner sometime?"

"Patrick, I'd love to. Really I would. But the fact of the matter is that I'm married. Married to a man who's married to his work. But married just the same," she said wistfully.

"Oh, the beautiful girls are always taken," Pat said with a half smile. "But if you ever decide to leave this jerk who doesn't have time for you, give me a call."

Pat wrote his number down on the back of his business card. As he handed it to her, his hand lightly stroked her palm and fingertips.

"Believe me, if that ever happens, you'll be the first to know," replied Rita. "But my husband…he…he's really a fantastic guy. He's just never around."

"Well, he just doesn't know what he has. I hope he doesn't let a good thing slip away."

"Yeah, me too," she responded. "Thanks, Patrick Kelly, for saving me from that creep. And for the water. Bye, Shep," she muttered as she strode across the yard.

Pat watched her trim silhouette move fluidly across his lawn and continued to watch as she jogged down the street and out of sight. Hours later, he still couldn't stop thinking about her. He wondered where she lived and how some lucky bastard didn't realize his good fortune, having a beautiful woman like her.

Rita returned from her jog and immediately took a shower. Not only did she want to rinse off the sweat of the run, but she wanted to wipe away her guilt. Deep down, she wanted to see Patrick Kelly again. Five Fifty-Five Seminar Drive was only eight blocks from her house. Although she desperately needed a friend, she shrugged off her thoughts of Patrick, grabbed a terry bathrobe, and went into the bedroom.

Chad was still asleep, his brown hair falling over his lean, handsome face. Rita laid beside Chad, listening to his steady breathing. But as hard as she tried to erase the events of that morning, Patrick Kelly's smiling face appeared every time she closed her eyes.

———

After Rita left Pat's house, he sat down and shook his head in disbelief. How could he be so interested in a woman who was unattainable? His

Catholic upbringing made him feel so guilty about his attraction to her. *Oh well*, he thought to himself, he'd never see her again. And if their paths ever crossed again, he vowed he would keep his distance. Maybe it was because he was on the rebound from Tracy, his former fiancée. And maybe he was still homesick from leaving his hometown of Hickory, North Carolina.

Pat had only been in Charleston for three months, and he didn't particularly like the city. Being raised in a strict Catholic home in Hickory, he loved his large family of five brothers and one sister. His father died when he was twelve, but his mother, Patrice, worked two jobs to provide for her children. With the small pension from her husband, Ted, she was able to manage on a strict budget. Pat had always been a whiz in math, but when it came time to attend college, he knew his family couldn't afford it. So he enrolled in a technical program for drafting, hoping one day he could afford to enter an engineering program.

He had just completed his drafting program when he met Tracy Jacobs. Tracy, a vivacious blonde, was a great complement to Pat's introverted personality. After a few months of dating, he bought Tracy a ring with a small diamond chip. On their next date, Pat took Tracy to their favorite restaurant, a small Italian restaurant named Vinny's on the south side of Hickory. After dinner, Pat cleared his throat and took the ring out of his coat pocket.

"Tracy, I know we haven't dated very long. But I know what I want, and now I want to spend the rest of my life with you. Will you marry me?"

Tracy looked at the ring, then at Patrick in disbelief. "Yes, yes, I will. I love you, Pat, with all my heart," Tracy replied, tears streaming down her face.

Pat slipped the ring on her finger, and the couple left the restaurant arm in arm.

After Pat and Tracy announced their engagement, Patrice Kelly had a family meal to celebrate their engagement. After all of the toasts and congratulations were offered, Patrice summoned Pat into the kitchen.

"Pat, you are my youngest, my baby boy, and I adore you. I am so happy that you are engaged, and Tracy is a wonderful girl, but…" Patrice stopped in midsentence.

"Mom, is this another one of your premonitions?" asked Pat, shrugging his shoulders in disgust.

"Call it what you like, but if you marry Tracy now, I think you will regret it. And you know I raised you that divorce is not an option for a good Catholic boy."

"Mom, I assure you… Tracy and I are in love, and the last thing I would ever think of is divorce."

"Well, just make sure your engagement is long enough so you both are sure about this," whispered Patrice.

Seven months later, Tracy called off the engagement. Pat had no idea why. She came up with some lame excuses, that she needed space and time to think about getting married. He wondered if there was another man, but didn't ask. Deep down, he didn't want to know.

So when his firm transferred him to Charleston, Pat felt secretly relieved. A new town and a new job might help him get over Tracy. He often thought of his mother's warnings about Tracy. But in his new house in Charleston, the loneliness seeped into every empty room. When he first moved in, he would pick up the phone and dial her number, only to hang up right before the phone rang.

But as Pat assumed the routine at his new job and settled into his home, he began to think less of Tracy each day. And as days turned into months, he started to realize that maybe his mother was right….maybe he and Tracy weren't meant for each other.

After he met Rita, he focused on work, trying not to think about this beautiful woman who had entered his life unexpectedly. The weekdays quickly passed, and Pat contemplated what to do on a Friday evening. On Fridays, he usually went to a bar called Clyde's to have a few beers. He had just showered and changed into a pair of jeans and a blue Polo shirt when his phone rang.

"Hello," said Pat, thinking his mother was on the other line.

"Hey, Patrick. It's Rita."

Pat's heart raced in his chest. He took a deep breath and said nothing for a few moments.

"Patrick, is this a bad time for you?" she asked, tension mounting in her voice. "I had your number from the card you gave me. Hope you don't mind I called."

"No, not at all. I was just getting ready to head out the door to go to Clyde's. Would you like to join me? And you can call me Pat."

"I don't think that would be a good idea," said Rita in a soft-spoken voice. She worked for an advertising firm, frequently encountering business acquaintances when in restaurants and bars. "I was just calling to say hi and wondering if you would ever want to get together and talk. I sure could use a friend, Patrick. I mean Pat."

"Sure, sure," Pat found himself saying. "How about dinner at my place Wednesday night?"

"How about lunch instead?" asked Rita.

"Lunch it is," replied Pat. "How about one?"

"Sounds good. I'll bring dessert. See you Wednesday for lunch, Pat."

"See ya, Rita. Watch out for those bad guys when you go jogging," he joked.

"Don't worry. Good-night."

"Night."

Pat didn't know what he was doing with Rita, but for some reason he couldn't resist. *Besides,* he thought to himself, *what harm could come from having lunch with her just once?*

———

On Wednesday morning, Chad kissed Rita good-bye at six o'clock sharp. She was still in bed, and he smiled as he kissed her good-bye.

"When will you be home tonight?" she asked. "What time should I have dinner?"

"Rita, I have two out-of-town deliveries to make. So I don't know what to tell you. But I'll be home just as soon as I can. I love you," he whispered.

Rita didn't answer. She turned away from him as he left the room, secretly planning a rendezvous.

———

Chad's life changed drastically the day he agreed to join his father's business. Gene Everitt had worked all of his life to build his small trucking company into a profitable venture. At eighteen, when Chad had the opportunity to attend college, his father had a heart-to-heart talk with him.

"Son, you know I could use your help. And you're my only son. Everything I have worked for will be yours," said Gene.

"What about Brooke?" Chad had always looked out for his little sister.

"We'll help her find some rich boy to marry. And when we do, we'll pay for a nice big wedding for her."

Somewhat reluctantly, Chad became his father's right-hand man. He was accepted to many universities, but turned them all down. His father reassured him that once they got on top of their bills, Chad could attend part time. But Chad's college dreams were never a part of Gene Everitt's business plans. The only thing Chad got out of the deal was a low weekly salary, a run-down frame house to live in, and a promise the business would eventually be his.

It was three years later when Chad met Rita. Even though he didn't attend College of Charleston, the school was only a few miles from his house. Sometimes he would amble through the campus on Friday nights and crash parties. But he usually felt so out of place; he would leave early without even making an attempt to converse.

It was the end of August when he decided to attend a campus party on a Friday night. Classes would be in session the following week, and he thought this might be a good time to meet some people. But what Chad really wanted was to meet a girl. He felt so isolated from everyone his age and wanted desperately to have a steady girl.

It was around nine o'clock when Chad arrived at a dorm where loud music was playing. He entered a smoke-filled room crammed with college kids, either with a drink in hand or puffing on a joint. This party wasn't his style, so he stood over in the corner and felt out of place. He decided to wait about thirty minutes, and then slip out unobtrusively.

Out of the shadows, a young lady approached him with a smile.

"Hello, cowboy, you look a little out of place," she said with a laugh.

"Yeah, I guess my boots gave me away. I stole away from the ranch for a few hours," he joked.

"Well, my name's Rita. And I'm glad you got away, even if it's only for a few hours." She looked him straight in the eyes. "What's your name, cowboy?"

"Chad Everitt. Nice to meet you, Rita," he replied nervously.

"Want something to drink?" she asked.

"Well, to tell you the truth, I wasn't planning on staying too long. Parties just aren't my style."

"So, Chad, what is your style?"

"Going someplace quiet to get to know you better. How about going with me to have some dinner?"

"I've already eaten. But I'd be happy to go along for some dessert. I know a diner about a block away that serves a great apple pie a la mode. Are you game?"

"Sure, just lead the way."

They walked silently, side by side. Chad could smell her jasmine perfume and watched as her long ebony hair swayed in the slight breeze. He stole glimpses of her toned body, how her waist curved in and led to voluptuous hips. Chad couldn't believe he was in the company of a beautiful woman, and he desperately wanted to impress her. But he was so shy around women; he felt at a disadvantage.

As they entered the diner, they took a seat next to the glass case where the desserts were displayed.

"That apple pie there sure looks good. Is that what you would like?" asked Chad.

"Sure, but while you eat your meal, I'll have a cup of coffee. But I'll be waiting to dig into that apple pie."

When the waitress brought Chad his meal and refilled Rita's coffee, the conversation died. Rita looked down at her coffee, while Chad cut into his roast beef.

"So, Chad, what is your major?" she asked, trying to make small conversation. She sensed Chad's shy demeanor. But this interested her even more. Most boys she met just wanted to talk about themselves.

"You first. What's yours?" he asked, trying to get the conversation away from him. If she knew he wasn't in school, she would lose interest.

"I'm majoring in communications. One day, I want to be a television journalist. At least that's my goal for now," she said as her green eyes widened in excitement.

"That's a great goal. And you definitely have the looks for television. You are beautiful. But I'm sure you get told that a lot," he added and looked away.

"No, not really. I don't date that much. And since I'll be graduating next May, I'm more focused on my career right now than a relationship. So…how about you?"

Chad looked down at the table and cleared his throat before he answered. "Right now, I'm not in school. I work in my dad's delivery business and will eventually take that over. But I will soon attend classes part time. I want to major in economics."

"Well, well, a business man. I admire you for wanting to get your degree. Make sure you stick to that," she said. "So, what brings you to the campus when you don't go to school here? Do you always crash college parties?"

"No, not very often. It's just that all of my friends are in college, and I really don't get to meet anyone my age, working all the time. So once in a while I get up enough nerve to come over here and see if I can find a party and try to meet a few people. I hope you don't think that's wrong."

"No, I think it's a good idea. It'll also keep you interested in attending school for yourself. Now I'm ready for that apple pie with two scoops of ice cream." She grinned at him.

Chad smiled back and gathered his courage. As Rita was finishing the last of her apple pie, he cleared his throat and spoke softly. "Rita, I was wondering if you would be interested in taking in a movie tomorrow night? We could have dinner first and then catch the late movie. What do you say?"

"Cowboy, I would love to. How about picking me up at six? I'm in Weston Hall on campus. Just come in the front lobby and they'll page me. But for now, I have to get back. I still have to unpack and straighten up my room. And I have the worst roommate ever. She is such a slob—I can tell that already."

As they left the diner and stood outside, Chad reached out for her hand. "Rita, I'm so glad we met. And I look forward to seeing you tomorrow night."

"Glad to meet you too," she replied and gave him a kiss on the cheek. Then she disappeared down the street.

After that first meeting, Chad and Rita became inseparable. They saw each other four or five times a week. After a few months, Rita moved in with Chad, which angered Chad's father.

At work, Chad had to listen to his father's rantings. "Chad, you kids don't have any business living together. You're too young to be settling down. Besides, you and me have a lot of work to do."

For Chad, all he wanted to do was work and make a comfortable home for Rita. When he worked, all he thought about was her. She was absolutely the most beautiful girl he had ever laid eyes on. After seven months of living together, he took her shopping for an engagement ring, on the eve of Rita's college graduation.

Rita's eyes were wide with excitement as she picked out a diamond solitaire that cost as much as Chad's dilapidated car. They put it on lay-away for three months, paying on it every single week. When they made the last payment, Chad took her to a cozy restaurant on the east side of town. He and Rita toasted to the future while the main course was cleared from the table. Then he went down on one knee and uttered softly, "Rita, I love you so much. All my hard work, all that I do is to try to make you happy. Will you marry me?"

"Chad, you don't have to get down on your knees. My money is on this rock, too. But yes, yes, I will marry you. I love you, too."

The waiter brought them dessert and coffee, while Rita stared at the brilliant diamond on her finger.

"We have some plans to make, cowboy," she said softly. "And don't think that I'm gonna do it all by myself. I'll need your help, too."

"Rita, whatever you want. You know that," he said.

Chad reached for the bill; cognizant he had to stand up to his dad. He knew he had to spend more time with Rita if he was going to make her happy.

———

With trembling hands, Rita turned the key of the ignition to her red Mustang convertible. Her dark hair blowing in the breeze, she drove the five blocks to 555 Seminar Drive. As she pulled into the driveway, she cautiously parked under the branches of a huge live oak tree. Content that her car was hidden from view of the street, she knocked on Pat's front door.

Visibly trembling, she was tempted to run to her car and not look back. Just then, Pat answered the door.

"Rita, so happy to see you. I didn't hear you knock. I was so busy fixing lunch. Come on in."

She entered the doorway, noticing a table already set with a navy blue tablecloth, wine glasses, and blue stoneware.

"Lunch smells delicious. But you shouldn't have gone to so much trouble," she said shyly. "Here's my small contribution to lunch." She handed him a chocolate cake, still warm from the oven.

"Sure I should have. I'm trying to impress you," he replied with a chuckle.

"Lunch is ready. Have a seat and I'll pour you a glass of wine. Red or white?" he asked.

"Chablis would be great," Rita replied.

Pat placed a salad bowl on the oak table and ladled out chili, while Rita sipped wine.

"Here I am, just sitting here, while you're doing all the work. But I must say it's nice to be waited on like this," she said.

"Well, enjoy it."

As they ate lunch, they made small talk about the weather and their work. Both had taken the day off to have this lunch date.

Once lunch was over, Rita suddenly felt the urge to leave.

"This has been nice. But I really should be going," she blurted.

"Why? You haven't even been here an hour. How about a game of Ping-Pong? I've got a table in the back room. I challenge you to a game," he urged.

"I'm really not that good. But what the heck?" she added.

The Ping-Pong game didn't last very long, as Rita wasn't skilled and Pat had plenty of practice. Rita laughed as she slammed the Ping-Pong ball against the wall.

"See, I told you I wasn't any good," she said with a laugh.

"Yeah, but you could beat me in a foot race any day."

"I'll bet I could too," she quipped. Glancing at her watch, she bolted toward the door. "This is nice, but I really need to get going. Chad will be home in a few hours."

"I'm glad you could come. Are you sure you have to leave so soon?" He stood in the doorway in front of her, blocking her path.

"Pat, this is wrong. I really shouldn't have done this. You know I'm a married woman," she replied, trying to convince herself more than Pat.

"The fact that you're here tells me you're not happily married," Pat retorted.

Rita didn't answer right away. Then she said, "You're wrong about that. Chad's a steadfast, honorable man."

"I'm sure he is," replied Pat. "I'll see you to your car."

"No need. I can find my way out." She kissed Pat on the cheek. "Thanks for a wonderful meal. Good-bye, Pat."

"Bye, Rita. Guess I won't see you again. But I'll tell you this before you leave. You're the most beautiful girl I've ever laid eyes on. I'd fix you lunch any day."

Rita drove away, thinking Chad had never washed a dish, much less fixed her a meal. With Pat, she had never been so pampered. All evening, as she made dinner for Chad and waited hours, as usual, for him to come home from work, she thought about Pat and the compliment he had given her. When Chad arrived after nine o'clock, she ate in silence, shaking her head as if to erase Pat from her memory.

When Chad went to sleep that night, she phoned Pat, and they planned a rendezvous at a remote resort in the mountains a few hours away from Charleston, for the following week.

Rita drove into the gravel parking lot in front of the wooden cottage. She glanced at her watch and gazed around nervously, as if someone might recognize her. This was the spot she had agreed to meet Pat for their secret getaway. A wave of guilt overcame her as she thought about Chad. Having second thoughts, she placed the key in the ignition to drive away. But as she started the car, she saw a set of headlights as Pat parked his black Dodge Charger next to her convertible. He flashed a toothy grin and dangled the key to the cottage in his hand.

"Never mind you've kept a lady waiting," she said.

"Oh, but I'm well worth the wait," he replied.

They entered the whiteboard cottage nestled in the woods, without saying a word. To their right was a small sign stuck in the grass: *Evergreen Row: White Cottage.* The small cottage seemed expansive because everything was painted white—the walls, the ceiling, the bedposts. A white ceiling fan hummed quietly atop the queen-sized bed.

Pat came toward her, slowly and deliberately, staring into her green eyes. He embraced her in a passionate kiss and slowly undressed her. His hands gently brushed her cheek, her mouth, and her breasts before kissing her again. Quickly, she undressed him, slowly joining his body to hers. For hours, they made love again and again. Rita was aware of the slow hum of the fan and the pure white of the walls that seemed to mesh their two bodies infinitely into one.

When their orgasms were over, they lay together, sweat pouring profusely from their bodies. Tears of joy rolled down Rita's cheeks. "This has been so beautiful. But yet so wrong."

"Rita, I want you to have this," he whispered. He opened a small box sitting on the dresser Rita hadn't noticed before. It was a gold ankle bracelet with a dainty diamond pendant draped in the center. He bent over her nude body and clasped it around her left foot, kissing her feet gently and making sure the anklet was secure.

"Pat, it's beautiful. Thank you."

Pat turned toward her, holding her gently in his arms. "Rita, you know it's against my religion to do what I'm doing. How do you think I feel? I know we just met each other, but I'm falling for you. If our relationship is to go anywhere, you're going to have to eventually tell

Chad about us," he replied firmly, a glint of fire flashing from his steel blue eyes.

"It's not that easy. Chad is a devoted man. But we--we haven't been intimate for a few months now. He knows that something is up. He's not stupid, and every time I leave, I see that hurt look in his eyes. I did take a vow to be with him. And then you...you come into my life. How could you?" she asked and hit his shoulder with a clenched fist.

"Rita, let's not ruin a good thing. Regardless of what happens to us, I want to remember this day forever," said Pat. And without any resistance, Rita surrendered into his arms again.

A few hours later, Rita kissed Pat on the cheek. "I have to go. Chad will be home in less than two hours," she said. "Enjoy the rest of your time in our White Room. Remember me," she whispered, feeling Pat's eyes imploring her not to leave.

Rita arrived home only a few minutes before Chad. She was cooking steaks and baked potatoes when she heard the familiar sound of Chad's footsteps at the doorway.

"Hello, Chad. Dinner will be ready in about thirty minutes," she replied, her heart beating rapidly. The lies and deceit were becoming part of her daily routine.

"Rita, just where have you been all day? I knew you had the day off and I have been trying to call since noon. I actually talked Dad into giving me the day off tomorrow, and I wanted to take you out of town. Thought we could go on a little romantic trip for tonight." Chad had a hurt look in his eyes, and Rita couldn't make eye contact.

"Where have you been, Rita?" he asked again.

"I've been out shopping."

"Who with?"

"By myself. But I didn't find anything."

Chad said nothing, but he turned away from her, grabbed a change of clothes and headed for the shower.

During dinner, they ate in silence. After Rita cleared the table, Chad came to her and kissed her. Right now, she felt no love for him, only pity. Yet, as if to prove herself a dutiful wife, she followed him into the bedroom, where they made love for the first time in months. When it was over, Chad turned to her, tears streaming down his face.

"Rita, who is he?"

"What are you talking about?" she asked, looking down at her pillow instead of his face.

"It's obvious you have a lover. Do I know him?"

"You're crazy. You have just been working too much. If you were home more with me, you'd know that wasn't true."

"Well maybe it's a good thing I don't know him. Because if I did know him, I'd...I'd." Chad stopped in midsentence, his fists clenched. Then he turned away from her sobbing in the darkness.

Finally, sleep silenced his crying, and all she heard was his steady breathing. Steady, dependable Chad. If only Rita could love him like he loved her. She felt sorry for Chad, but in the back of her mind, she thought about Pat in the White Room all by himself, wishing she were still there with him.

For the next few months, Rita saw Pat as often as she could, making excuses to Chad concerning her whereabouts. As she drove to 555 Seminar Drive on a chilly January afternoon, little did she know it would be the last time she and Pat would make love. As usual, she entered the back parking lot and parked next to his car. Their signal was three loud knocks on the door, followed by two more.

Pat came to the door, his curly hair disheveled. "Come in, Rita."

They sat on Pat's lumpy couch for a few minutes, stumbling through awkward conversation.

"How did you manage to get away today?"

"I told him I had to return some clothes that didn't fit and I might stop in at Jerry's for a drink afterward. He didn't like it, but he didn't say anything."

"Rita, I can't go on like this. My mother wants to come down for a visit and wants to meet you. Ever since she talked with you on the phone last week, she has loved you and keeps talking about how she thinks I've met the right person. If she knew—"

"Well, what do you suppose that we do?"

"Let's not see each other for a while. You go home to Chad and try to work things out. If you decide once and for all to leave him, then I'll be here. That way, we'll be doing the right thing, the right way, in the right order," he said.

"Pat, in case you haven't noticed, it's too late to do things the right way," she replied sarcastically. Then she turned his face toward her and kissed him slowly, digging her hands into his shoulders.

He gingerly picked her up from the couch and carried her into his bedroom, where they made love feverishly.

Rita left Pat's around eight o'clock that evening and then stopped by Jerry's Bar and Grille for a quick glass of wine. Even though it was little consolation, at least part of her story line to Chad would be true.

When she pulled into her house about an hour later, Chad was already home.

As she entered the dimly lit living room, Chad was sitting on the sofa, staring idly into space. When she sat next to him, he turned away from her. Visibly, his body shook.

"Why, why, Rita? Why are you doing this to me?" he asked.

"Doing what?" she responded. "I told you I had some shopping to do and then I was gonna stop by Jerry's for a drink. You can call the bar up, and somebody there will remember me if you give them my description."

"Oh, I'm sure someone there remembers you all right," he added. Tears began to roll down his cheeks. "Rita, I work so hard just for you. Christ, you're all I think about all day. I can't wait to get home to see you every day. I know it's been hard on you because I'm not one of those guys who enjoys dancing and going out a lot. But you know how much I love you and I…I have never lied to you. Not once. I don't think you can say the same to me."

Rita didn't reply at first. She just hugged him tightly as he struggled to regain his composure. "Chad, I'm here with you now, aren't I?"

"Are you *really* here with me, Rita?"

Chad broke away from her arms and stumbled toward the bedroom, banging the door shut behind him.

For the next several weeks, Rita slept on the couch, waking up early and going to work an hour ahead of schedule. She avoided Chad as much as possible because she couldn't stand the hurt look in his eye. Pat called her almost every day, but she refrained from returning his calls. She had to make a decision: end her marriage, or forget Pat and make her marriage with Chad work.

Rita hadn't seen or spoken with Pat for two weeks. Even though her body ached for him, she tried to focus on work. On Wednesday morning, Rita happened to think her period was two days late. She really didn't worry—she was often late. But when she was a week late, a feeling of dread shadowed her every waking thought. Chad asked her why she was so quiet, but she blamed it on being tired. When two more weeks passed, her nipples became sore and she felt nauseated in the morning. Then she knew.

She went to a nearby pharmacy and bought a home pregnancy test. When the pregnancy test confirmed her suspicions, she locked the bathroom door, rocking back and forth on the floor, biting her lip and fighting back the tears.

For two days, she dialed Pat's number and hung up before he could answer. On the third day, she found the nerve to call him and stay on the line until he answered.

"Hello," she heard Pat say nonchalantly.

"Hey," she replied, her heart beating so fast, she felt it pulse in her head. "I really need to talk to you. Soon," she stammered.

"Rita, I miss you so much. But as long as you're with Chad, I can't keep doing this. I want you all to myself."

"Well, there's something I need to talk to you about. It's really important. As soon as possible," she added.

"Is this about you leaving Chad and moving in with me?" Pat asked, excitement in his voice. "But please, don't give me false hope."

"What I have to tell you will definitely change everything," Rita answered. "But I can't talk about it now. Chad's about to come home, and he doesn't know what I'm about to tell you. How about tomorrow night?" asked Rita.

"I'll be home by five. How about six at my house?"

"Sounds good. See ya then."

The next evening, Rita phoned Chad at work to say she was going to a friend's house and would be home by nine.

Chad mumbled something under his breath, said he'd be working late, and hung up the phone.

Rita drove to Pat's house, her mind jumbled with thoughts.

As she drove down the dusty driveway, she glanced around to see if Chad had followed her. Satisfied that she was alone, she knocked three times on the door, followed by two taps, their secret signal.

Pat came to the door, running his hands through his dark brown hair. He opened the door without saying a word, motioning her in with a wave of his hand.

Rita sat on the couch, and Pat sat next to her.

"So, what's on your mind?" he said, his blue eyes piercing through hers.

"There's no easy way for me to say this," she stammered, looking away.

"Is this about Chad? Did he threaten you?" he asked protectively.

"No, this has nothing to do with Chad. Pat, I'm pregnant," she burst out, tears running down her cheeks.

"Rita, are you sure?" he asked.

"Yes, I'm sure. I haven't been to a doctor, but I did a home pregnancy test and it was positive. And...well...I feel different...nauseated in the morning."

"I know just when it happened," replied Pat, shaking his head in disbelief.

"It happened the last time I came to your apartment. And I want you to know there's no chance that it's Chad's," she whispered.

"Rita, don't worry, I believe you. But what are you going to do?"

"I don't know. I'm very confused and in a state of shock right now."

"Rita, if you were free, I would want to marry you," he said, his eyes a steel-blue commitment to the future.

"I just need some time to decide what I want to do. I wasn't expecting this. I didn't plan on this to happen," she stammered.

"Well, once you make your decision, let me know. I'm here waiting, as always," he replied. He looked so uncomfortable, wringing his hands and not knowing what to say.

"Well, I have to go." Rita choked out the words, tears streaming down her face. She somehow didn't feel welcome now, even though they had planned to have dinner together.

Rita reached to hug Pat good-bye, but he turned his face away. He motioned toward the door.

"Like I said before. Call me when you know what you want. It's either me or Chad. If you leave Chad, you know I'll take care of you and the baby."

"You said you'd take care of me. But do you love me, Pat?" she implored.

"I'll do right by you, Rita."

Rita nodded through tears, found her way out the door and sat in the parking lot for several minutes. As she sobbed, she thought about the White Room and all of the memories of stolen moments with Pat. But Pat didn't say he loved her.

What a mess she had made of things. Fighting back the tears, she had to feign composure. In just a few minutes, she would be turning into her driveway. Her house. Chad's house.

That night, she made dinner and kept it warm on the stove. Chad arrived shortly after nine o'clock, appearing pale and listless as he walked across the living room.

Chad rarely drank, but he went straight to the refrigerator and opened a beer.

"Want one, Rita?"

"No, I'm fine. I'll have dinner on the table in a few minutes." She needed to stay busy, fix dinner, wash dishes, clean the whole house, all the while wishing the life within her would leave spontaneously.

Chad sat in his usual place at the table, watching her suspiciously.

"So, why are you home so early? Is he out of town, or what?" Chad asked, a sad expression on his face.

"Just what are you talking about, Chad? I went to see an old friend. I left early so I could be home and fix dinner for you."

"Yeah, an old friend. Rita, I love you so much, but I'm not dumb. I realize I haven't been the best husband. I've been married to my work, trying to please my dad too much instead of you. But I can change, I swear. I love you so much." He bit his lower lip until it bled. "I would die for you. Christ, Rita, how could you do this to me, to us?" he screamed.

"Chad, I don't need this right now. I need your support. I'm here for you right now, aren't I?" she replied.

"Not really. You haven't been here for me in months!" he said, leaving the kitchen and slamming the bedroom door as Rita stood helplessly in the middle of the kitchen floor.

———

For a week, Rita contemplated what she wanted to do about the pregnancy. Meanwhile, Chad acted like their fight had never happened. He talked to her about going out of town the following weekend, but she refused.

The following Monday, she made an appointment to have an abortion. But when she entered the clinic, she sat across a woman with a small child. The beautiful little girl with blonde ringlets toddled around the room, flashing Rita a broad grin. Rita jumped up and ran from the room. Hastily, she drove away from the abortion clinic. That day, she knew she wanted to have the baby.

But as the days passed, she realized the dilemma this baby would create. She was married to Chad, and legally he was the father of the child. If she kept the baby, Pat would demand she leave Chad. But Pat didn't love her.

Still, all she thought about was Pat's piercing blue eyes; somehow she knew the baby she carried had those same striking eyes. How could she destroy a child created out of such passion? But if she had the baby, her life with Chad would be destroyed. And if she chose a life with Pat, she would always be the woman who led him away from his strong Catholic beliefs. Guilt would always be there; eating away at any relationship she and Pat could ever build.

She decided she'd tell Chad about the pregnancy. If she were to have any chance of reconciling with him, she had to start telling the truth. At least half-truths. After dinner Friday night, she cleared the table and then cleared her throat.

"Chad, there's a reason I've been acting strangely lately. I'm pregnant."

"You are? Really? Rita, that's wonderful," he exclaimed. Rita couldn't tell if he was being sincere or sarcastic. Didn't he have a clue the baby might not be his?

"No, Chad, it isn't. You and I have a lot of issues to work through before we have a family. I'm not ready to be a mother," she replied.

"Well, what do you want to do?" he asked innocently.

"I don't know. But I'm thinking about…about not having it." The word "abortion" was too ugly to utter.

"An abortion? Are you sure?" he asked.

"No, I'm not. I just need you to give me support and give me time. I want us, just you and me to work on getting our marriage where it needs to be. And to do that, you and I need to spend some time alone."

"Rita, you've done things I don't understand. And I don't understand this. But my mom and dad would be thrilled to be grandparents," he said.

"But I need to be thrilled to be a mom. And right now, I'm not."

"Fine! Fine, you'll do whatever you want to do anyway. You always do. But I have a say in this too," he yelled.

Rita was on the verge of telling Chad about the affair. But the risk of losing someone so steady and true was too great to take. She held her tongue and said nothing.

Another week passed. Reluctantly, Rita made another appointment. She believed if she kept this baby, she'd lose Chad. And she felt she'd already lost Pat.

The day of the appointment, she refused for Chad to go with her. Even though it was recommended that someone drive her home, she knew she was strong enough to go through the procedure by herself. After all, she only had herself to blame for the mess she had created.

As she lay on the gurney, a nurse started an IV and did a vaginal exam. Then a doctor entered the room and started the procedure. It was then Rita knew she had made a horrible mistake. She felt like she was being raped from the inside as the machine sucked out the life of her unborn.

Before the doctor left the room, he uttered, "It's over."

In so many ways, it was.

In recovery, a nurse examined her, as Rita sobbed uncontrollably.

"You were farther along than we thought. You were about thirteen weeks," the nurse stated.

"No, that's impossible. I know when it happened," Rita replied, sobbing into a crumpled tissue.

But the reality set in--- now she didn't know who the father was. Instinctually, she believed Pat was the father. But now, it didn't matter. A life had been terminated that day. And no matter what she did, she could never get back what she had thrown away.

After the abortion Rita went into a state of depression. Refusing to take the recommended days off from the advertising firm, she immersed herself into work to forget about what she had done. The thought of killing her unborn child made her feel unworthy of living.

Chad was very supportive. He brought home carryout for dinner and tried his best to boost her spirits. But seeing Chad made her feel even more guilty and more unworthy. He was so steady and devoted. Conversely, within a few months, she had managed to ruin her marriage and create a messy situation for Pat.

It was a few weeks after the abortion when the phone rang at four o'clock in the afternoon. Rita debated on whether or not to answer the phone, but decided on the fifth ring to answer it.

"Hello."

"Rita. Hi. I've thought about you a lot the past few weeks," said Pat, sounding distant on the line.

"Yeah, I'm fine. Really."

"I was wondering what you decided to do. I never heard."

"It's taken care of. It's over," Rita replied, trying to hide the pain in her voice.

"I wish I had known. I would have been there for you," he exclaimed.

"It's OK. I went by myself. No big deal, really," she lied.

"Well, Rita, I really need to see you one more time," he said.

"Where? How? When? Do you think it's really a good idea under the situation?" Rita asked. She didn't know if she could handle seeing Pat.

Her heart was breaking at the thought of seeing him again, stirring up old feelings. Feelings she knew were forbidden after the choice she had made.

"Meet me at six at Flannagan's. Tomorrow. How does that sound?" he asked.

"The sooner the better. See you tomorrow. Don't be late," she joked.

"I never am," he replied. But his voice sounded strained. Deep down, Rita knew she had already lost him.

Rita arrived at five thirty and chose a table in the back. She couldn't risk seeing anyone from Charleston she knew. If someone from the advertising firm saw her with Pat, she'd have to deal with petty office gossip. She sipped coffee while she waited for him, rehearsing what she'd say when he arrived. Suddenly, she thought about the only conversation she'd had with Pat's mother.

"Rita, I can tell from your voice that you are a wonderful lady. I'm hoping you're the one for Pat, the one who'll make him happy. If you're that girl, I'd welcome you into our family."

Rita came back to reality as someone tapped her on the shoulder.

"I had a hard time finding you here in the back," Pat said.

"You know me, I always played hard to get," she joked.

Pat ignored her joke and changed the subject. "I need privacy to tell you what I need to tell you. Can you follow me to my car?" he asked.

Rita paid for her coffee and followed him into the familiar leather interior of his car. He drove without saying a word, to a park nearby. In full view, children were playing on swings and slides. Rita turned her head. Right now, the sight of small children was unbearable, reminding her of the life she threw away.

Pat cleared his throat and spoke softly, looking around as if someone had followed him. "Rita, I feel really bad about everything. If things were different, I would want to marry you," he said.

"But, now...now you don't. You couldn't even if you wanted to, could you? What I did was a sin," she said, with tears welling up.

"What's done is done. You have Chad. Me, I don't have anyone to turn to. But I have a responsibility to you. Here's my half of the procedure."

Pat had five hundred-dollar bills in a wad. He shoved it toward her lap. "I want you to take this."

Rita threw the wad of money in his direction. The bills scattered like sheets of paper in the wind.

Pat picked them up and placed them atop Rita's open purse. "Rita, don't argue. That's my half. I was part of this, too. It was wrong, but I was part of it," he stated.

"Wrong. Is that all we were?" she sobbed. "Don't you understand? I ended this pregnancy because I was so confused. I ended this pregnancy so I'd have a chance to think this situation through, to see if I was meant to be with you or Chad. Chad is such a compassionate man and I do have feelings for him. Then I met you and it seemed so natural we should be together. But now that I've done this, ended this pregnancy, you can never forgive me, can you?"

Pat didn't answer. He just nodded. "Rita, this was all wrong. Deep down, you know," he replied.

Slowly, Rita removed the ankle bracelet from her slender foot, the only tangible gift he'd ever given her. At least, the only one she hadn't destroyed.

"No, you keep it. It's yours," he said, waving his hands emphatically.

"Well, *you* might not feel like this. But the White Room was a beautiful night," she said.

"It was *wrong*," he insisted firmly, as if he were at confessional.

"Well, I guess this is it, isn't it?" asked Rita.

"Yes, Rita. Good luck to you and Chad." He started the Charger and drove her to the restaurant parking lot. She left his car, slammed the door and didn't look back.

For weeks, she was stunned. Trying to forget someone like Pat was hard to do. Knowing patient, steady Chad was there for her every night should have helped. But she kept thinking about Pat and his clear-blue eyes and how beautiful their baby would have been. She dialed his number several times but hung up before he answered.

About two months after their breakup, she saw him for the last time. She was on Interstate 26, heading east, while Pat was heading west in the opposite lanes of traffic. As they passed, she caught sight of him, wanting him to turn back, to turn toward her. But he was gone, forever out of sight.

The following week was the second week of May, and a gusty wind was blowing as a thunderstorm brewed in the distance. As she left her house for work, Rita had the ankle bracelet in her hand Pat had given her. Running late as usual, she decided she'd strap it to her ankle when she arrived at work. She held it tightly as she headed to her car. When she opened her clenched fist, the ankle bracelet wasn't there. She backtracked her steps to the house, but the anklet had vanished.

When she came home from work that day, Chad asked her if she had made the right decision about the pregnancy. Like a wounded child, she shrieked and shook her head indecisively.

Chad was consumed with questions he wanted answered. Was the baby his, or did she even know? But never again would he ask her what happened.

A few months later, Rita heard rumors that Pat had reconciled with his former girlfriend, married her, and moved somewhere in the Midwest. It would take time, but Rita came to understand that when the bracelet disappeared, it was a sign she was never meant to be with Pat. Chad was her steadfast, faithful husband. Every day, she prayed to love him half as much as he loved her, to end forever this yearning for someone, for something she had lost forever.

———

Years later, Rita wakes up covered in sweat. She is dreaming of a blue-eyed infant that shrivels and dies right in front of her. This baby, the only child she would ever conceive. The baby she destroyed. But when she has this recurrent nightmare, she turns in bed toward Chad. And he is always there to hold her.

"Rita, another bad dream?" he asks.

"Yes, dear. But it's over. For now," she says as she turns away from Chad and stares into the darkness that will forever encompass her.

FOURTH OF JULY

As the fireworks display begins, I feel the tight grip of my mother's hand, while the dark night sky suddenly brightens with dazzling light. *Pop, pop.* One brilliant display after another, white stars dance and dart across the sky. Bright red and blue rockets shape the horizon before falling harmlessly before us. My hand hurts from my mother's death grip on me, but I cannot wrestle free.

In the dim light on the back porch, I turn to face my mother. Unlike the fireworks' bright lights in the sky, I see only shadows when I look into her eyes. A blank look, the light reflecting but not penetrating.

"Mom, that's a pretty one! See it?"

"Yeah, really nice, hon. Where are we again?"

And I tell her for the third time in the last ten minutes.

She smiles. "How nice for Nancy to have us."

We are *not* at Nancy's house.

A sweet memory suddenly overtakes the reality of the evening. The fireworks display is set to begin. My mother's strong hand holds mine, as the twilight shadows envelop the crowd. *Pop, pop.* One brilliant light display after another. White stars dance and dart across the sky. Fireworks in shapes of patriotic flags and stars streak across the blackness. Then they fall harmlessly to the ground. I try to wrestle free from my mother's protective grip on my hand, but I cannot. I am five years old, and it is the first fireworks I can remember.

Today, I think back on who my mother was. She was black coffee, Doublemint chewing gum, and bright red lipstick. She was energy, warm embraces, laughter, and jokes. But today, she is none of those things. She is silver hair, a blank stare, trembling hands.

And I think…she is like the fireworks. Once dazzling, lighting up the night air. Now, the neurons in her brain, like the fireworks, slowly burn out. One by one, slowly, mercilessly, they are extinguished.

GAVIN

He is standing over me, screaming at the top of his lungs. My firstborn. The only child to survive within my womb. I had fought so hard to have him, went against my doctor's orders to conceive again.

You could die if you tried, the doctor said. And yet I suffered through months of unbearable pain for the miracle. He was perfect. Or so I thought forty-two years ago. Thinking back on it, I was forty-one. Almost his age. And he's screaming at *me*?

I hear his angry voice pounding into my skull, feel the spit from his vehement lips on my cheek, see his fists clenched in rage. And I cannot move. I cannot speak. But I can hear. I can feel. And now, how I wish that I could yell back, tell him how selfish he's being. Tell him...tell him...anything. Anything at all.

"Why did you go through all of the money? My inheritance? Where is it? Why are you in so much credit card debt? And now, I have to take care of *you*?"

He sits down next to me in a faded-blue chair adjacent to my bed. But his screams still reverberate in my head.

A burly nurse comes in to check on me. "Is everything OK, Mrs. Tanner? Mr. Tanner?"

"Everything is fine. Fine," Gavin says.

The nurse checks my feeding tube and catheter. How I wish she would give me a lethal injection so I could be out of the way. Out of Gavin's way.

Gavin, more calm now, after his explosive rantings, tells me good-bye. Yet he still lingers, looking at me like I am an object not worthy of respect. I want to hate him, but I only pity him. One day, if not for the grace of God, he might be lying in a bed like me. No power. No motion. Only thoughts. Scattered, fleeting. But thoughts just the same.

Several hours after Gavin leaves me, I realize I'm lying in my own excrement. I try to will my finger to move the call button on my bed.

Why do they have a call button on this damn bed when they know I cannot move? It is useless to try. I am stuck in this reality of pain, devoid of dignity.

The searing pain shooting down my legs fades as Tom's face suddenly appears before me, an apparition of years ago. Tom and me together on our wedding day. How handsome he looked, gazing into my eyes as we exchanged vows. But the promise of our wedding day soon faded into years passing without a child. Feeling barren, unwhole. Knowing people looked at me with pity.

The thoughts of Tom don't last long because again, Gavin appears at my bedside, screaming at the top of his lungs, still demanding infantile attention. I try to tune him out. His face is so close to mine, I can feel his anger. Yet I do not know if Gavin is an apparition or a reality. I blink my eyes to try and look away from his face, blood red with anger. If only I had the strength to cover my ears from his shouts so loud they seem to penetrate my skull. Mercifully, the sedatives the nurse gives me suddenly kick in and I sleep.

When I wake up, Gavin is gone. Images from the past creep into consciousness. Faded thoughts, like spent blooms on my rose bushes in the hot August sun. Thoughts about Gavin when he was a baby.

———

After Gavin was born, I was ecstatic. He was so perfect, so healthy. I remember how he looked at six months old, with dark ringlets and deep brown eyes. I doted on his every whim. He was my focus, my pride and joy.

When Gavin was a toddler, Tom would talk to him about hay bales and cattle and tractors, while Gavin would listen intently, as though he understood every word. As soon as Gavin could walk, Tom would occasionally take him in his battered green ton truck. From the tattered seat, Gavin would gaze at me on the front porch. I would sit in the porch swing, nervously rocking back and forth, holding my breath for his safety.

I imagined Tom returning Gavin to me, shredded to bits by a hay baler or crushed by a tractor. But Gavin always returned to me with cheeks flushed from the breeze through the truck's open windows, his brown eyes aglow with excitement from the adventures. I felt estranged from my husband and son, never sharing in these adventures.

But most mornings, as Tom would leave for his farm work at the break of dawn, he would quickly hand Gavin to me. And those mornings, Gavin would scream at the top of his lungs for Tom. I would hold him, against his will, until Tom's truck puttered down the driveway, out of sight. Gavin would cry, kicking and screaming for Tom, making me feel small, unloved, and worthless.

While Tom worked on the farm, I was confined within the walls of the small white frame house. I'd spend my time washing Tom's dirty bib overalls, coated with diesel and cow manure. When the laundry was finished, I scrubbed dirty dishes and dingy floors. But each day, I would allow myself the luxury of a cup of tea and a chapter from one of my favorite books. Whether it was *Jane Eyre*, or *The Great Gatsby*, it was always the best part of my day.

The morphine mercifully allows me to sleep for a few hours. I cannot move my eyes to see the institutional black clock on the wall, but when the nurse enters to check my catheter and IV, and all of the machines hooked up to me, I can only assume it's in the middle of the night.

Another nurse joins the first, making the comment, "She looks pretty good for someone semi comatose and terminal. I've seen worse."

I've seen worse. That's what Tom said about me when we were alone and he thought I couldn't hear.

But it wasn't always that way. Tom was one of the last available bachelors in Carroll County. All the single women knew he was handsome and would inherit his father's five-hundred-acre farm. At the age of thirty-three, most of his friends already had wives and babies and a paunch for a belly. But Tom was lean and tanned with a broad smile, his bright-blue eyes creased from hours of baling hay in the hot summer sun.

I met Tom one night at an annual square dance sponsored by the Daughters of the American Revolution. Tired from decorating the fire hall all day with red, white, and blue streamers and red balloons, I debated on whether or not to even attend the gala. An hour late, I nervously sauntered into the dance hall. As the dancing began, I sat alone, sipping on punch, hoping no one would notice how I had shoved my chunky body into a blue satin dress designed for a girl much prettier and thinner than I would ever be.

Tom walked toward my table, but I never dreamed he'd stop. The food table was to my left, so I assumed he was making a beeline for the hors d'oeuvres and spiked punch. I had been watching him all night as he danced with every available woman in the room. But when he approached my table, he stopped right next to me, leaning in my direction. I could smell his after-shave and breathed it in. *What do I do now? What do I say?*

"What's a pretty girl like you doing all alone at a dance?" he asked with a smile. "Do you mind if I sit for a minute?"

Before I could answer, he plopped down next to me.

"You've been dancing with all the pretty girls. You must have me mixed up with someone else." *Why did I always say all the wrong things?*

"You just need a little confidence, Ellie Lawton. I've been trying to get the nerve to talk to you. I see you every time I check out a book at the library, you trying to hide behind your thick glasses. But I see the beauty you're trying to hide."

I blinked and nodded nervously. No one ever talked to me that way. I had only been on a few dates in my life. At thirty-one, I assumed I would be an old maid, destined to live out my life in this small town. My identity was cemented as the old maid county librarian and a silent member of the Daughters of the American Revolution.

The music began for the next dance, and Tom didn't even ask. He grabbed my hand and led me across the dance floor. Holding his large calloused hand in mine, I looked up at his tanned farmer's face and smiled. For the first time in my life, I felt attractive and special.

Tom and I were married three months later, much to the surprise of every other available female in the county. I could hear their whispers when we walked by.

"How did Ellie Lawton ever hook him? He could do a lot better. Must have been her inheritance money."

How I tried to ignore the idle gossip. I silently wondered if there was any truth to the naysayers. My mother and father died in a car accident when I was twenty-five. As an only child, I inherited a small frame house and twenty thousand dollars from their estate. And as a dutiful wife, money I shared with Tom after we were married.

With the negative comments in my head, I tried to lose a few pounds. But nothing would ever change my large frame. Tom insisted I was a strong, beautiful country girl, a perfect fit as a farmer's wife. He talked about having a big family and a couple of boys to work on the farm. I told him I wasn't a spring chicken and we'd better get started soon.

———

When we were first married, Tom seemed to be bursting at the seams in love with me. He beamed whenever I walked into the room. He couldn't wait to get home and off his tractor to see me. He would sweep me off my feet, carry me to the bedroom, and make love to me.

I was a devoted wife. So devoted, I even sold my parents' house and put the proceeds into Tom's farm account. Now my inheritance was all gone, spent on farm equipment Tom needed, or so he said. But I couldn't give him what he really wanted. A son. Month after month we tried, but nothing happened. Waves of depression about my infertility overcame me. I quit my job at the library as soon as we got married, so for days on end I saw no one but Tom. When I did go into town to get supplies, I could hear the whispers behind my back.

"Poor thing. Can't have a baby."

Or "Poor Tom Tanner. Married a homely woman who can't even give him a child. Who's gonna get the family farm? Strangers?"

I'd pretend not to hear the idle talk. Sometimes I'd wish for my old life in the library. I missed the smell of books. I missed being in control of the library, checking the books in and out. Seeing the local folks. Carrying on intelligent conversations about authors and titles. And now I knew Tom didn't really love me. After four years of marriage, Tom would leave in the morning without speaking to me. Every morning, I woke up at five a.m. to fix him a full breakfast. Eggs and sausage. Biscuits and gravy. And on Sundays pancakes and syrup, with bacon.

No. Tom didn't love me anymore. Maybe he never loved me. He loved what he thought I could give him, an heir to the farm. And the money I had inherited from my parents to keep his farm afloat.

Although I desperately wanted a child, I stopped feeling sad every month I didn't conceive. My fortieth birthday came, and Tom forgot it. It totally slipped his mind, and I didn't remind him. I'll never forget that day. He was working his usual sun-up until sundown on a crisp fall day. I baked a chocolate cake (his favorite, not mine) and decorated it in red, white, and blue. Just like the decorations the first night we had danced at the DAR party.

After supper, I brought out the cake, about to place forty candles on it, the candle box hidden in my apron pocket.

"Why'd you make my favorite cake, Ellie? You know Doc Brown is telling me to lose weight." He jerked his chair away from the table and went upstairs, leaving me alone. Tears in my eyes, I put forty candles in the cake and watched as they burned and the wax melted onto the fudge frosting. Forty years of life and nine years of marriage. And what did I have after all of that commitment? A chocolate birthday cake and no one to share it with. No one to remember why I even had a cake.

I slowly lost all hope of ever having a child. Tom never spoke about it, but when we were together in public, at church on Sundays, or walking about in our small town, his eyes were always drawn toward children. During these moments, I felt small. I seemed to disappear into the cracks on the sidewalk, and Tom didn't even miss me. Tom and me, together but so alone. All because we wanted the same thing and I couldn't give it to us.

"There goes Mr. and Mrs. Tanner. It's too bad about Ellie. She can't have kids, ya know. And Tom wants a boy so badly. Someone to leave the family farm He just married her cuz she had a little money in the bank."

But then one month, the miracle happened. Without warning, one spring morning, a wave of nausea hit me. I thought it was a case of the flu, but when it happened two days in a row, I happened to think that my period was two weeks late.

Thinking I was going through early menopause, I didn't even consider I might be pregnant. But when I began vomiting in the early morning, I joyfully realized a new life might be growing inside me.

I hid the news from Tom. I wanted to be sure. Not wanting to get his hopes up or mine. I had suffered two miscarriages in the past and didn't want to endure dashed hopes again. Both times I miscarried, Tom looked at me as if something was wrong with me. His stares seemed to make my barren womb an open visible wound that never healed.

So I sat in silence over dinner night after night, while Tom smacked his lips together and ate whatever I cooked, while the thought of eating made me nauseous.

One night he looked up from his plate of steak and mashed potatoes and poked me in the ribs. "What's wrong with you? You look white as a sheet. And you barely touched your food. You need a dose of iron tonic?" he said with a grin, and pointed to the bottle of Geritol in the cabinet.

I ignored his coarse comments, quickly washed the dishes, and retired to bed early.

The day I went to Dr. Adams and told him I was pregnant, Doc obviously doubted my story. No one knew better than Doc Adams I couldn't possibly have a child. And Mrs. Adams, the gossip of Carroll County, made it the talk of the town.

"Well, let's see when we examine you," he said as I was sitting in the stirrups, shivering under the sheets. As his gloved hand entered my vagina, probing, he appeared in deep thought.

"My dear, I'm shocked. But…yes, I would say you're about eight weeks along. But we need to talk."

"About the pregnancy? I know I'm probably high risk at my age. But Tom and I—"

"I know Mrs. Tanner how much you want a child. But at your age, you're at higher risk for something to go wrong with the pregnancy. Plus, you have adhesions on your uterus. You may still abort the pregnancy, like you have before. And you're at a higher risk for hemorrhaging when you deliver. I think you should consider terminating this pregnancy. It's for the best."

"No, no, I won't even consider that option. Tom's always wanted a child. I've always wanted a child. I'm willing to take the risk."

After I saw Dr. Adams, I couldn't hide my pregnancy from Tom anymore.

"Are you sure?" Tom asked over and over, as I told him the news on a cool spring day.

I kept nodding, bobbing my head from side to side, and grinning like a Cheshire cat.

Doc Adams warned me about the risks, but I didn't realize my life would be in jeopardy every day I carried Gavin. The bleeding started in the third month, a hot July day. During my pregnancy, Tom made dozens of trips to the hospital, with me propped in the back of the old tan station wagon, wondering if I had lost another pregnancy, bleeding profusely. Three different blood transfusions in four months.

I lay flat on my back in bed for most of the pregnancy. Knowing the feeling of lying in my own pool of blood, wondering if I would live to become a mother. Wondering if I would ever know the joy of holding my child. Wondering if I could ever please Tom by giving him an heir to the farm.

Tom would visit me at the hospital and wring his hands. Deep lines creased his forehead and gray hair appeared that wasn't there before. But he never voiced his fears. Or his love for me.

They took Gavin early from my diseased uterus, or he and I would have both died. As I came out of the anesthesia, I saw him. The answer to my prayers. Gavin. So perfect. So pink and healthy. Gavin screaming at the top of his lungs, demanding attention.

———

Gavin comes every morning to see me at the hospital before he leaves for work. Since we lost the farm, Gavin works at the stock sale every Tuesday and Thursday. He also helps out Dale Winter, one of our neighbors, on his cattle farm. Today, Gavin doesn't speak about how it's my fault we lost the farm or how much debt we're in. He just sits quietly by my bedside, watching my tired eyes flutter helplessly around.

Watching all of the tubes and monitors. Watching me slowly die.

When the doctor enters my room during his rounds, I overhear the doctor speak of my death.

"Gavin, it may be this week. Or it may be two or three months. One never knows how long someone wants to hang on."

Hang on? To what? To whom?

Gavin, my only son, my only family member still alive, wants me dead.

I am ready for this agony to end. Strapped to a hospital bed, hours pass slowly. Nurses come and go, checking on my lifeless body.

I feel water and a washcloth on my body. Sensations of rough hands on a towel. Then cold lotion dabbed on my feet and hands. Even the slightest touch causes extreme pain.

The nurse turns me on my side.

"Poor thing," she utters. "It'll all be over soon."

Another nurse enters the room. "Did you look at her chart? Her liver's failing."

Talking about my death as if I'm not even in the room. As if I can't hear. I should feel relieved. My agony should be over in a few days. Maybe hours.

But I want Gavin to be here. I want Gavin to not yell. I want Gavin to do something he is incapable of doing. I want him to love me.

———

Gavin stopped loving me the day Tom died, when Gavin was a senior in high school. Maybe he blamed me. Well, maybe it *was* my fault.

On a crisp autumn day, Gavin was getting ready to leave for school when his father came in from the barn. Tom strode through the kitchen and headed for the bathroom. I could hear him fumbling through the medicine cabinet.

"Ellie, where's the Pepto Bismol?" he yelled. "That lousy breakfast you made me has gave me indigestion. My chest is hurting from the acid."

I ignored his plea to find the Pepto Bismol and busied myself with washing the dishes. The hot water burned my hands, but nothing ever hurt more than Tom's insults.

"Mom, are you sure it's indigestion? Dad looked awful pale when he came in," Gavin said with concern in his voice.

"He always gets indigestion whenever he eats too much. You go on to school. I'll keep an eye out for your father."

"OK. Thanks, Mom," he said as he sauntered over to his truck, leaving Tom and me behind in a cloud of dust.

That was the last time Gavin ever thanked me for anything. As he drove off to school, I heard a thud in the bathroom.

"Oh, no!" I screamed.

I rushed to the bathroom, and Tom was laying on the floor, gasping for breath, his eyes blank.

"Tom! Tom! Wake up," I screamed.

But I couldn't wake him up. Panic stricken, I ran to the kitchen phone to call the rescue squad. When I returned to the bathroom, Tom was not breathing. I wept silently, lying next to him. Tom was dead. I knew he was dead. I did not need the ambulance workers or a doctor to tell me. His eyes were open in a blank stare.

Gavin met me at the hospital. When he arrived, he didn't know his father was dead. I asked the doctor to tell him. As he heard the news, Gavin did not cry. He showed no emotion while the doctor was in the room.

The doctor asked if he had any questions. Gavin said he had just one.

"If my mother had called the rescue squad when my father first complained of chest pains, would he still be alive?"

"That's something we'll never know. But he suffered a massive heart attack. So probably not. It's better not to think about that, son. Your mother needs your help right now," stated the doctor tersely.

Gavin saw tears streaming down my checks, but did not console me. Anger was in his eyes as his body shook with rage.

"Mom, are you satisfied now that Dad is dead? You were always jealous of how close we were."

The days following Tom's death, I got no help or support from Gavin. He stayed in his room, looking at pictures of his Dad. He and his dad on tractors. He and his dad at the county fair. Pictures where I was never included.

During the funeral, everyone in the county came, or so it seemed. All of the ladies who talked about me behind my back were the first to express their condolences. Even at Tom's funeral, they whispered loud enough for me to hear.

"Poor thing. Ellie Tanner will never hang on to the farm. And Gavin, why, he'll have to give up on going to college."

"Ellie doesn't know beans about running a farm. What on earth did Tom ever see in her?"

———

Life without Tom was more difficult than I'd ever imagined. I didn't have to cook greasy meals or smell cow manure on gumboots or wash dirty bib overalls. And I sure didn't have to listen to Tom's demands and insults. But I missed him. What I missed most was how he'd pat cologne on his face some Saturday nights after he'd taken a shower, and cuddle next to me, his massive arm around my waist. Those were the times I tried to remember—not the times he belittled me or looked past me to connect with Gavin.

I tried to maintain the farm, just like Tom would have wanted it. I had promised him, and I always kept my promises. At least until this one.

Many times in the past, I had asked Tom to teach me how to do things—how to run the tractor, how to tend to the cows. But he always said that wasn't my place. Gavin would run the farm if anything ever happened to him.

Gavin tried to keep the farm together, but he lacked Tom's work ethic and business sense. Little by little, we had to sell off the farm to pay the taxes. When Gavin wanted to plant corn and soybeans to keep the farm acreage we had left, I gave him the last of my savings. But that year, we had the worst drought in forty years and lost our entire crop.

That's when the bankers called in our debt, and we were forced to sell all but five acres around the house. Five acres and a rundown farmhouse. The bank couldn't take that from me. Our homestead. Enough for me and Big Red, our prized bull, and one heifer. That's what I wanted. But Gavin had other plans. He decided to sell all of our livestock, including Big Red, and despite my protests, put his plan into action.

Gavin helped our neighbor, Joe MacGrady, load the cows and pigs and chickens while I stood on the hilltop under the willow tree. The willow tree where Gavin used to play. The willow tree where Tom kissed me the first time I saw the farm. The willow tree where Tom proposed to me and made me feel loved and wanted. But today the willow tree offered me no solace, while a bitter north wind burned my face.

As they were loading the last of the cattle, the bull refused to load. "Big Red," as Tom called him, had sired our entire herd of Hereford cows, the best herd in the county, everyone said.

Gavin and MacGrady lashed Big Red until he was gashed and bloody. Still he would not load. Big Red snorted and thrashed around the small pen.

"Guess we'll have to shoot him," MacGrady commented dryly. "I can't waste all day with him. I'll go get my rifle."

Gavin nodded, glaring up at me.

I decided for once in my life, I'd take a stand. Lumbering down the hill, I screamed at the top of my lungs. "Stop! Leave him be."

"What in hell are you doing, Mom? You don't know a thing about this. Get out of our way."

"I still own this farm. And you will do it my way. Leave Big Red alone, or I'll call the sheriff."

MacGrady exited his dusty Ford pickup, rifle in hand.

"Are you sure, Mrs. Tanner? All of these animals are headed for the stock sale. Probably end up at the slaughterhouse anyway."

"Stay out of this, Mom. I'm just glad Dad isn't here to see us lose everything."

"We haven't lost everything yet, Gavin. You have no trust in me. But no one touches Big Red. He's a part of this farm. As long as I own a little piece of this farm, he'll be here. And leave the last heifer here too, to keep him company. I'll take care of them."

Gavin sneered and slithered into Tom's truck. My truck now. But Gavin had already taken control of it. Like he was trying to take control of everything else in my life.

Big Red ran up the hill, under the willow tree where I had just been. The heifer followed him, just like I had blindly followed Tom during our entire marriage. I figured Tom was looking down, knowing I did the best I could.

———

I don't need the nurses telling me my liver was failing. My body feels weighed down, probably from the fluid. I imagine my skin turning yellow and jaundiced from the poisons building up in my system.

Gavin arrives sometime in the evening. I hear his voice, but I can't understand every word.

"Mom...I...could...talk...you."

I imagine he is crying, but know that's impossible.

On and on he rambles. I hear babbling.

"Why...you...leaving......way?

I attempt to fill in the blanks, believing that he is sorry, that he regrets how he treated me all these years. All these years.

———

Gavin moved into town the day they auctioned off the farmland. When the auction gavel fell that day, Dan O'Brien, the wealthiest farmer in Carroll County, bought our land. Soon after the sale, Dan plowed under our pastureland and planted corn and sorghum. Tom probably rolled over in his grave the day the plow pillaged our pasture.

Gavin still worked for the farmer down the road, Dale Winter. But he never came to see me. Sunday after Sunday, I fixed a meal for two and ate alone, hoping Gavin would come.

I didn't talk to my own son for more than twenty years. Every week, I wrote him a letter and he never responded. Every week, I called him and he hung up when he heard my voice. Every Sunday, I hoped to hear his truck drive down the dusty driveway and hear his raucous voice.

But one doctor's visit changed all that. I hadn't felt well for months. The pain throbbing across my chest came and went. I assumed it was angina and ignored it. My legs would sometimes swell, and I could barely walk.

After several days, I asked Mrs. MacGrady for a ride into town to see a doctor. What I didn't expect was the concerned look on old Doc Brown's face. Two weeks and tons of medical bills later, I was diagnosed with leukemia. With no health insurance, I was forced to put the house and five acres up for collateral. I wrote to Gavin and begged him to come and see me. But no word.

Did he know I was sick? Surely he knew.

Every neighbor in Carroll County knew, so Gavin had to know. The neighbors brought casseroles and cakes and plates of food I never touched.

I was losing everything and had no one to share the losses with. No one who cared. I had two credit cards to my name I rarely used. But to pay for my chemotherapy, I used them to the maximum credit limit.

But the chemo was like poison to my body. It didn't stop the leukemia. The white blood cells kept getting higher, and the red blood cells lower. I needed a blood transfusion to stay alive, so the neighbors got together and had a fundraiser for me. While I was in the hospital receiving the blood transfusion, the banker came and foreclosed on my house and the five acres. He asked Gavin to haul off my personal belongings.

Gavin never told me about losing the house and the remaining farmland. An old friend of mine from the library, Cora Smith, dropped by the hospital to give me the news.

I had already lost Gavin. But losing my aged Big Red and my home was more than I could bear. I promised Tom that if he passed before me, Big Red would die of old age on the farm and I would never lose the farm. That Gavin would have the farm after Tom and I were dead and gone. Those were all promises I couldn't keep.

Right after Cora left, I remember feeling numb on my left side. I couldn't speak; I was so frightened. I tried to ring the call bell to notify the nurses, but my brain was shutting down. I tried to scream, but no sound came out.

A few minutes later, a nurse found me, lifeless. She conducted CPR and saved my life. Why I'll never know. Why didn't she let me die? That's when my weeks of torture began, trapped inside a distorted zone of pain and suffering. And knowing there was no one on this earth who loved me.

———

Slowly, one by one, the nurses are shutting down the tubes and machines that are keeping me alive. A doctor is overseeing their work of ending life.

Gavin has ordered it. He is legally in charge. Not me. I was never in charge.

My only child is in the shadows. Gavin, who refused to see me for over twenty years, is here to end my life.

I feel myself slipping away and see an apparition of Tom in his bib overalls beckoning me toward him. Fighting to the very end, I open my gray eyelids slightly and see Gavin, bent over me, whispering something.

"I... loved Dad...Mom." I hear, "...sorry for...nothing... done."

What was in the middle I never heard, as I shut my eyes for the last time, floating away into oblivion.

SECOND CHANCE

A young woman slowly walked down the gravel road on a chilly March morning in 1986. Paltry sunlight filtered through bare trees that lined the edges of the vacant country byway. No one was there to see the pain in her eyes, or how her jaw was set, her face covered by a white silk scarf fluttering in the icy breeze as she faced the north wind. Her long thick hair hadn't been combed for two days and hung in knots, hiding her ghost-like face. She shivered under her heavy wool coat, partly from the cold, partly from the illness, but mostly from fear.

Diana walked down the steep hill and heard the creek roaring under the low water bridge. In March, the creek was always high. Pausing for a minute, she thought about the day she almost drowned in the swimming hole, right there by the bridge. She was only three when she waded out too far on a warm August day. Her big brother, Rich, had saved her. He deftly jumped in the creek, pulled her out, and dragged her to the safety of the creek's rocky edge. She thought about that day so long ago and wondered why she'd been spared.

She contemplated stopping there, checking her coat pocket for its contents. Already tired and out of breath, her face was distorted in pain. Gazing in the mirror that morning, she hadn't recognized the person staring back. A face that radiated health and beauty just a few months ago looked tired and ashen today. A body taut and muscular now strained for the energy to pull out of bed and face another day. She was tired... tired of not knowing what was wrong, and tired of doctors telling her nothing was wrong. But mostly she was tired of doctors telling her she was crazy. Well, maybe she *was*. But the sickness, whatever *it* was, had made her go crazy.

Diana paused briefly at the bridge where her brother had saved her so many years before. Impulsively, she pulled her coat sleeve up to her elbow and looked at the scars on her right wrist, three thin lines about two inches in length. She had gripped the razor and tried to slit her wrists, but when the stinging pain hit and the blood started dripping, something made her stop.

Her head was pounding as it had every day for months. She was in constant pain, but no one seemed to understand. Her feet were numb and her heart was racing as she decided to walk a bit farther to the next bridge. As she walked alone, she passed neighbors' houses without any feelings of nostalgia. It was too painful to think about pleasant memories past. She knew what she must do, what she had wanted to do for months, since the day she was taken with the sickness.

But no one believed she was sick, not the doctors, not her husband, not her sister, and certainly not her mother. Her husband had given up on her, said he couldn't take care of her. He sent her home to be with her mother, thinking that was what she needed. She cried the day he drove her there, begging him to understand she really was sick. Regardless of what *they* said, it had *nothing* to do with her brother. Everyone thought she had fabricated the sickness, to feel his pain.

Just a few months ago, she had walked into a sporting goods store and bought a shotgun. It seemed surreal, dark, and menacing to even hold the gun in her trembling hands. She hid it in the closet and waited until her husband was gone. Then, somehow she lost her nerve. With a shaky hand on the trigger, her weakened arms tried to lift the barrel to her head. Instead, she accidentally shot a hole in her closet floor, piercing the living room ceiling below. She remembered the smoke and the fire from the gun and hated herself for not having the nerve to aim the gun at her head and have it over, the pain, the suffering, and the not knowing.

Her husband took the gun away, unaware she had a spare, what she called her "second chance" at slipping away. She had taken her favorite ring—a garnet stone set in gold—and traded it for a pistol with a pearl handle. The man at the pawnshop with the crooked tooth and greasy hair handed it to her gingerly.

"Ma'am, do you know how to use this?" he asked politely.

"It's for my protection. My husband is gone a lot," she lied.

The pistol remained in her Tennessee home, hidden in a drawer where her husband would never look. It was miles from her mother's house in North Carolina, but somehow it comforted her to know it was there. Just the thought of gripping the pearl handle with her shaking hand somehow soothed her. It was eerie; she used to hate guns. Now the only thing that made her feel better were thoughts of her own self-destruction.

As Diana walked on, she thought of her brother, Rich. Everyone believed her sickness began the day she knew he was dying. But her sickness was real, just like the AIDS virus destroying his immune system. He told her his secret, how he had one lover too many in a gay bathhouse years ago, and made her promise not to tell. And she kept her word, had not told a soul—not her husband, not her mother, not anyone.

A few weeks after her brother's shocking revelation, she started having headaches, and numbness in her limbs. She lost part of the vision in her left eye and couldn't keep her balance. When the fevers started, they were never high enough to cause alarm, just enough to make her ache and drain her energy. The doctors tested her for everything. They first said she had a virus. If she didn't know better, she would have thought she had AIDS. Even though she knew she couldn't contract it from her brother, the thought had crossed her mind. Then the blackness overcame her brain. She couldn't read, couldn't concentrate, and couldn't remember what she had last said or done. Diana knew her brother needed her, knew her husband needed her, but most of all, her two small children needed her. But she had nothing to give. She couldn't run, couldn't laugh, and couldn't move without pain.

When she first arrived at her mother's house, right before Thanksgiving, she anxiously awaited a visit from her brother, somehow hoping he could lift the darkness from her brain and she would get better. Her brother came to see her, his face pale, but his body still strong. She admired how he always walked and sat with perfect posture, his steel-blue eyes gazing into her face, seeing his pain reflected back into her own.

When she told him she was sick and felt like she was dying, he gave her no pity.

"Sis, at least you have a place to die. Me, I have next to nothing," he calmly replied and changed the subject.

Shortly after Diana arrived at her mother's house, her mother tired of her daughter's constant care. During the Christmas season, her mother sent her away, committed her to a nearby psychiatric hospital. She was sedated and treated with heavy doses of Haldol until she was drawn into a fetal position, unable to move. But no matter how many drugs they gave her, the darkness and despair still permeated her being.

Her doctor would make his rounds, always telling her she wasn't physically ill. She would argue, complain of her fevers and her headaches and her left eye that didn't seem to focus. She held firm to her convictions that she had a physical illness, all the while hoping to find a razor or a bottle of pills to end her misery.

David, a fellow patient on her floor, sometimes knocked on her door after dinner. Around and around the narrow corridors they would walk together. But sometimes David talked about hearing voices and needing his medicine, his voice screeching in the thin hospital air. Nurses would sound the alarm and take him away as he'd scream about death and destruction. Then she would climb back into bed and wait for the drugs she was forced to take before bedtime. They'd give her Haldol and a tiny cup full of Benadryl to make her sleep. But she'd often wake up, her arms drawn tightly around her body, rocking back and forth in bed.

Sometimes at night, she'd think about her family and what it was like before she was sick. She remembered holding her children on her lap and sitting on the front porch swing, while her husband mowed the grass on warm summer evenings. But those visions quickly dissipated and she somehow knew these moments could not be recreated. She felt unworthy of experiencing pleasure or love from anyone ever again.

Mornings were torture. Each day after breakfast, she would go to group therapy and not say a word. Diana yearned to leave the hospital, where she knew no one understood her sickness and her suffering. No one, except insane David.

Then one day, she realized a bitter truth. The only way she could get out was to go along with the doctors. So Diana lied to the doctors and agreed with them. No, she wasn't really physically sick, she'd say. She admitted to the hospital staff she had a psychiatric disorder and needed help. The doctors then smiled and nodded knowingly to themselves. When she began talking in group sessions about her "problems," the doctors knew she was on her way to recovery. Satisfied with her progress, they sent her home, still under heavy sedation.

It was a cold January day when she left the hospital. A crust of dirty snow lay on the frozen ground as she struggled to walk the short distance from the icy sidewalk to the confines of her mother's warm car. She breathed in the cold air and felt it burn her lungs. For just a second, she felt happy to be alive, to see the trees' bare limbs shaking in the bitter wind, and to walk down the sidewalk without a nurse's constant watch.

But a few minutes later, the deep despair descended upon her again. Her body seemed to disappear into the front seat of her mother's car. She didn't have the strength or the will to resist the forces that were plunging her into a dark chasm of melancholy.

Her mother briefly gazed in her direction as she drove. "You haven't even asked about your husband or your children. What are you thinking about? Don't you know they are hurting, too? You know, Rich told me about his illness. I know you two are close, but do you think you have to experience everything your brother does? Is that what this is all about?"

Her mother's words cut her deeply. She bit her lower lip until she thought it might bleed. Not answering her mother, she sank lower in the seat and rested her head on the door handle. As her mother drove in silence, she thought about jumping out of the car. Then her mother wouldn't have to care for her and she wouldn't have to feel the emptiness inside anymore.

———

After her release from the hospital, the days seemed endless at her mother's house. Diana searched for balance in her daily routine, but her mind was racing. Routine conversation was difficult for her. Even reading, one of her favorite past-times, was almost impossible. She couldn't comprehend what she was reading. Mostly, she just sat quietly, or lay in bed.

One afternoon in February, her brother came to visit her. He was coughing deeply, appearing thin and frail. One look in his eyes and she knew his pain, knew there was nothing she could do to save him, yet also knew there was nothing she could do to save herself.

"Sis, why is this happening to you?"

She looked in his clear-blue eyes and couldn't believe he was dying and yet remained so concerned about her well-being.

"What do you mean?" she asked innocently.

"Why'd you buy that shotgun? You're a coward. If you really wanted to die, you'd have pulled the trigger. Me, I'm trying to buy myself some time and you're trying to destroy whatever time you've got. It just doesn't seem fair."

"Well, I thought you of all people would understand," she said faintly.

"Sis, just remember what I tell you today. Life is tough. But you have to keep putting one foot in front of the other as long as you can, until you can't anymore. That's all I'm doing."

He began coughing violently, a deep, hoarse cough, and murmured his good-byes, leaving her despondent and alone.

Days were endless in her mother's small house. She would stumble down the narrow flight of stairs in the morning, feeling weak and brittle. She imagined herself as a bird left behind by the flock, weak and defenseless, wanting to take her last breath.

So each day, she watched television without really seeing anything. She ate what was placed in front of her, talked when she was spoken to. But mostly, she sat listlessly, longing for a way to end her misery. Sometimes her husband would call from Tennessee. And when he did, she would try to listen as he spoke of his day at work and how the two boys were doing. But it seemed dreamlike, almost as if their life together had never really happened. Visualizing her children playing at their grandmother's feet instead of her own, she wondered if she would ever hold them again. She couldn't muster the energy for love or emotion. So she chose not to think about them too often.

She knew everyone felt she was selfish—selfish for being sick and for being an unfit mother and wife. And knowing she had disappointed her family made her feel even more worthless and unfit to live. Quietly, she bided her time, hoping to earn her mother's trust.

On this windy March day she finally got her chance. She asked her mother if she could take a walk by herself. And to her surprise, her mother consented.

"Have a nice walk. Be sure to wrap up warm. It's really cold today," her mother said, not looking up from the breakfast dishes.

That morning, she walked about a mile from her house to the second bridge. Childhood memories again flooded her mind, memories she could not suppress. Long ago, the hot concrete from this very bridge had touched her bare feet, then the contrast of cool water as she plunged knee deep into the rocky creek, laughing in sheer childish delight.

But it was time to put those fond memories aside and focus on what she had to do right now. She climbed down the steep edge of the low water bridge, hidden from view by massive concrete tunnels. This was a perfect place. She sat for a few minutes; taking comfort in knowing this was where they'd find her, a place where she and Rich used to play.

She heard a car drive by and waited patiently until the car's engine could no longer be heard. Her hand clenched tightly around the bottle she had in her right coat pocket, the one she'd taken from her mother's bathroom cabinet just that morning. Thirty pills were in that bottle. She figured that would be enough to end her pain. So slowly she opened up the bottle, looked up at the sun one last time, and then swallowed them all.

For some reason, she changed her mind; she didn't want to be found by the bridge. She'd walk home if she could and then go to sleep in her bed at her mother's house and never wake up. As she walked the mile back to the house, she felt no ill effects.

When she entered the kitchen door, her mother was sweeping the kitchen floor. Suddenly, she felt herself fading. But it wasn't peaceful; it was a horrible sinking feeling, worse than any despair she'd ever felt. At that moment, she knew she'd make a terrible mistake.

"Mom!" she screamed. "Help me! Help me! I just took thirty pain-killers. I don't want to die!"

Her mother looked at her in shock. "Just what do you want me to do about it? What can I do? Tell me what to do! Oh no, Diana, what have you done?"

"Help me throw up. Give me something. And call the doctor!" she screamed.

Diana staggered in the bathroom and desperately tried to throw up. Her mother brought her a drink that tasted like vinegar, and she started throwing up the pills. But objects in her sightline started vanishing into shadows. Like snow on a television set, her vision started fading away.

"Mom, I'm dying. Please help me. Don't let me go to sleep. If I do, I won't wake up."

"You're starting to turn gray. Hang on—please—please don't leave me, Diana. I'm calling 9-1-1 right now." Her mother finally grasped the dire situation.

Diana hugged the bathroom commode and vomited more of the pills she had swallowed. Then the rescue squad came and took her away. At the hospital, they gave her some chalky liquid to drink, and she continued to vomit.

A nurse appeared in and out of her vision.

"You're lucky," the nurse said matter-of-factly. "It was too late to pump your stomach."

"Am I going to be OK?" she asked.

"Yes, you're going to be OK. But you are going to feel sick for several days."

The nurse left her room, only to reenter with several doctors who hovered over her like vultures examining a dead carcass.

"We are transporting you to another hospital facility. You are being committed to a psychiatric unit where you can get the help you need," stated one of the doctors after the examination was over.

"But I'm fine now. I don't want to die anymore. Please don't do this to me," she pleaded.

"It's not that easy, I'm afraid. Your mother has already signed the papers."

"But how can she do that?" she cried.

"Your mother has power of attorney. But you already knew that. This is not the first time you've been sent away." His tone was cruel, all-knowing.

Diana wept en route to the psychiatric hospital, more than an hour away. She was weak and drowsy, but was afraid to fall asleep, believing she'd never wake up. For the first time in many months, she felt grateful to be alive.

When she arrived at the hospital, they stripped her naked and gave her a mint-green hospital gown.

"When can I go home?" she asked. "And please, please don't give me Haldol."

"That's up to the doctor," said the nurse emphatically.

The nurse put restraints on Diana's arms and tied the fetters to the hospital rails. Against her will, she was restrained for several hours until she saw the doctor.

The doctor was young and handsome, and Diana cowered away from him, like a wounded animal.

"You are a very lucky young lady. Your liver and heart are perfectly normal in function. You're lucky you don't have any permanent damage."

Initially, Diana ignored him. She pondered what her mother said when she had begged for help, when she realized she didn't want to die.

"Doctor, please, please don't give me medicines. They make me feel so woozy and nervous and shaky inside. I don't feel normal when I take them. Please," she pleaded.

"Well, we'll try," was all he would say. Then he abruptly left her room.

That night, Diana was given drugs against her will. Although the medications were supposed to make her sleep, she tossed and turned. She finally dozed off, only to awaken a few hours later covered in sweat. This was the first of many nights she'd relive her walk from the bridge to her mother's house, her walk back from the grips of death.

During the first few weeks at the psychiatric hospital, Diana was under constant surveillance, still considered suicidal. Stripped of her dignity, she stayed in her room and stared at the walls for hours. It was during these first few weeks that her brother called. He sounded well, joking and laughing. He wanted to know why she was crazy. She didn't think it was funny and hung up on him.

He immediately called her back. "Don't hang up on me, sis. Hell, we're all crazy. At least you have a roof over your head and food to eat."

"Rich, I'm sorry for—"

"No. Sis, don't apologize. For those who understand, no explanation is necessary," he interrupted.

She wanted to respond to him, tell him she loved him, that she was grateful for his understanding words. But the drugs had numbed her senses. The tense silence between them seemed to freeze the telephone lines. Their conversation was strained, even awkward. She hung up after a forced good-bye. In bed that night, she lay awake dripping in sweat; her eyes wide open trying to face her demons.

Her recovery was slow and unsteady. She still tried to convince the doctors she had a physical illness. Even though she kept having low-grade fevers and infections, the doctors kept telling her nothing was wrong. Knowing no one really understood her in the hospital, she sat speechless in group therapy.

On certain days, she would sink back into a deep depression. Sometimes impulses would strike her brain about suicide. On one occasion, she tried to stick a bobby pin in an electric socket, but all it did was throw out a spark that frightened her. When the nurses heard about this incident, they sedated her and kept her under constant watch.

Through long days and seemingly endless nights, Diana started to improve. She began talking in group therapy, and little by little her meds were reduced. To pass the time, she went to visit fellow patients. Louise, a nervous housewife in an unhappy marriage, became an ally. They shared harmless jokes about their husbands, laughing hysterically.

Mercedes was an elderly, frail woman who always had a smile for everyone but rarely left her bed. Diana wondered what could be so wrong with a person who outwardly seemed so happy. Thinking about her own condition, she realized Mercedes probably hid her inner suffering.

In early July, her husband, Stuart, came to see her. His chestnut brown hair was disheveled even though he was immaculately dressed in a pinstripe suit. He approached her with a broad smile and kissed her on the cheek. "My dear Diana, we are lucky to still have you. I'm so happy you are improving." He flashed his brilliant smile, the pearly whites made even brighter by private visits to the curvaceous blonde dental hygienist.

When she saw him, she wanted to feel something, just a touch of the love they had shared. But she felt nothing.

She was granted a hospital pass for the evening, and Stuart took her to dinner in a cozy restaurant a few miles from the hospital. She hated the small talk, hated to answer his questions she knew he would ask about her recovery. Stuart was an attorney and seemed to always be in cross-examination mode, even with Diana. She ate forcefully, rapidly, secretly wanting to be back in her hospital room, alone.

"You're going to be discharged soon, probably in a week," he announced emphatically. *How did he know this and she didn't?*

She sat in silence, staring at her salad plate.

"Aren't you happy about that?" Stuart questioned her.

"Yes, yes of course. It's just the meds I'm on, they dull me, make it hard for me to feel anything."

"Listen, after you're discharged, I think it's best you stay with your mom for a while. I have to work, and I can't look out for you. Besides, I think it's in the children's best interest if you get a little better before you have to care for them. My mom's really helping out with the boys. I don't think I could have gotten through this without her."

Stuart spoke softly, but his jaw was set like a steel trap. Diana felt herself sinking back into a dark hole, faceless, nameless. No one, not even her own children, really needed her. She clutched at her chest and took a deep breath.

"'I'm really not feeling well," she said, choking on the words. "I need some fresh air."

After dinner, they walked the palely lit streets around the restaurant without touching or speaking. Stuart impatiently looked at his watch and motioned her toward the rental car. He drove several miles outside of town, down a quiet country road, where they made love for the first time in months. Only she didn't feel anything. She felt taken against her will and wanted this physical act to end.

Afterward, Stuart told her he loved her, that he couldn't wait until she was well enough to come home. And when the doctors said she was ready, he'd bring her home. As they approached the hospital, Stuart reached for her hand. Walking the short distance in the parking lot, Diana tried to keep up with Stuart's brisk strides. She felt out of time, out of touch with her husband. Past the nurse's station for check-in, they finally reached her room. Out of breath, she gratefully sank into her bed. Stuart kissed her on her cheek, said a hasty goodbye and was gone.

———

The next week, Diana was discharged from the hospital. She was anxious to leave, but afraid of what might happen next. Ironically, it was her brother, not her husband, who came to pick her up.

"Why, this is a surprise," she mustered faintly. But she was secretly relieved. For some reason, she felt safer with Rich than anyone else. Like no one else around her, Rich was completely honest with her.

She was dressed in jeans she couldn't get zipped, so she wore a big red shirt to hide her protruding belly. The combination of her medications and lack of exercise had left her fifteen pounds heavier than when she'd arrived. Her face looked bloated and lifeless.

"Sis, you don't look so good," Rich replied honestly.

"Try being in this hellhole for almost four months, making footstools and doing dumb-ass crafts," she replied. "The only thing I have to show for my time is a medical bill that will take me years to pay, and this footstool."

She pointed to the dark wooden footstool. For days on end in the craft room, she attached braided rope onto the sturdy oak frame. She would later realize this activity was the turning point in her recovery. For the first time in over a year, she was able to keep her mind on a task to completion. Deep down, she was proud of this footstool.

"Well, let's pack up and get Miss Kitty the hell out of Dodge before the posse comes after her," Rich said, chuckling.

As she and her brother left the confines of the hospital, the sun was scorching hot and painfully bright. She briefly wished she were back in her solitary hospital bed, sheltered from the outside world. She lugged her bulging suitcase down the massive concrete steps at the side door of the hospital. Two nurses smiled wanly and waved good-bye.

"Take care and be sure to take your meds. We don't want you to end up back here again," the nurse on the left stated bluntly.

Diana nodded and waved, turning her back on the nurses. Stiffly, she walked in the sweltering heat. Her blue jeans and red shirt were already dripping with sweat.

As they approached her brother's black Volkswagen Rabbit, she frowned.

"I sure hope you have AC," she thought out loud.

"We'll just roll the windows down and crank it up to about eighty five. That'll get a good breeze going," he teased.

She stared long and hard at her brother. He actually looked pretty good. Rich had gained some weight, and color had returned to his face. But right below his eyes, his cheeks looked sunken and hollow. She wanted to ask him how he was feeling, but refrained.

"So, sis, how does it feel to be out?"

"Good. Really good. I just want to get off these antidepressants. They've made me gain weight, and it's weird, I feel drowsy yet jittery at the same time. "Are you taking me home? I mean to Tennessee?"

"No, I'm taking you to Mom's. At least for right now."

"Rich, I want to go home, to my boys. I'm just a burden on Mom right now."

"Well, you're supposed to have constant care for at least a few weeks. Then we'll talk about a little drive to Tennessee."

"How have you been?" She finally got the nerve to ask him.

"Well, I'm still here, if that's what you mean. I was in the hospital a month back, some rare pneumonia. But I survived. Let's change the subject."

She drew in her breath. While she was fighting her demons, hoping for a chance to take her last breath, he had been fighting to stay alive. She shook her head in disbelief at the injustice of their situations.

An hour later, he turned onto the familiar gravel road that led to their mother's frame house. When he pulled into the lane, he suddenly stopped.

"You know, I tried too," he said.

"What are you talking about?" she asked.

"I took this car as fast as it would go. I must have been driving close to a hundred. After that bout with pneumonia, I didn't think I could go on. I figured if I made the next curve in the road, I was meant to be here a little longer. So I guess that's why I'm still here. It just wasn't my time."

Even though the heat was oppressive, she shivered as she turned to her brother, her chin quivering. "I know I hurt a lot of people. And I'm sorry for it. But I don't want anything to happen to you."

"Let it go, sis. Just forget about what I just said."

He took off, spinning gravel in a cloud of dust around them. When they reached their mother's house, he refused to go inside. He just waved to her and grinned broadly as she reached the front door.

"Call me, sis. Let me know when you can leave. We'll plan that road trip to Tennessee."

Abruptly he was gone, leaving her to think about him alone in that car and what might happen.

She walked into the tiny living room, where her mother was sitting reading the newspaper.

"I wasn't expecting you until later. Where's your brother?" her mother asked, rising from her chair to greet her.

"He couldn't come in. Said he had an appointment," she lied.

"Well, have a seat," said her mother stiffly. "So, how was the trip over the mountain? I know your brother drives like a maniac."

"You have no idea," she replied, thinking about her brother's most recent revelation.

"I don't understand why he doesn't get a job."

"Why, Mom, don't you understand? He's very sick. The AIDS is progressing."

She knew Rich had disclosed his illness to the family. Still, she thought about her promise, the secret she'd kept from everyone until this very moment.

"Yeah, well, the doctor said he was lucky to pull out of it. I know he had pneumonia. But he's fine now. He doesn't have AIDS any more than I do. He's more able to work than me, at my age, a widow keeping up this big house by myself," she snorted.

"You're wrong about him. He's really sick. As for me, Mom, I know I have been a burden on you, and I'm truly sorry. But right now, I think it's best that I go home to my family as soon as I can."

"Yeah, well, I think so too. But I'll do my best by you, until you're ready."

That night, Diana lay on crisp white linen sheets and began to feel the numbing effects of her medication. Before she retired to her room, her mother had carefully handed her two pills out of the bottle, watching her carefully as she swallowed them. Then her mother locked the pill bottles in the medicine cabinet, away from her daughter's reach.

The pills should have made her sleep, but instead she dozed in and out, seeing frightful pictures in her mind. She dreamed of her dead body floating away from her brother's emaciated frame. He was bleeding from every orifice, grasping to touch her hand one last time. But they never connected. She was overhead and ethereal, already gone from his reach. Waking from this nightmare, she tossed and turned in bed, unable to fall back asleep.

She turned on the night lamp and found her cherished picture album on the shelf in the corner. She thumbed through the familiar family pictures until she found the picture she wanted. There she was as a child, sitting on her brother's lap. They were laughing, looking right in each other's eyes as only siblings can, sharing secrets. She wondered how much longer she'd have him, how much pain he'd have to endure until the end.

The next morning, she tried to call her brother, but he was not home. Desperately, she stayed on the line as his phone rang and rang. When she finally hung up, she secretly vowed she'd visit the local library. Maybe she could do some research on experimental AIDS treatments. But for now, she knew of no drug, no hope for her brother.

Her mother went to get the mail, leaving her alone for a few minutes. Then the phone rang.

"Hello," she said hesitantly, hoping it was her brother's voice on the other line.

"Laura," the woman's voice said, thinking it was her mother. "How are you?" the woman asked.

"This isn't Laura. She went to get the mail. May I take a message?" Diana politely replied.

"Well, missy, are you satisfied now that you tried to kill yourself? Just think of all you've put your dear mother through."

The phone went dead with a loud click.

Diana wanted to shed a tear for the harsh remarks, but she couldn't. Her emotions were dulled, maybe from the medication, or from lingering depression. When her mother returned, she let her know someone had called and what was said.

Her mother looked sheepish, as though she knew who had called.

"Well, just ignore it. I'm just glad you're better".

"Someone is angry at me, that's for sure," Diana retorted.

———

After two more weeks at her mother's house, Diana finally arranged to see a different doctor. He agreed to slowly reduce her medications, acknowledging the side effects she experienced. For the first time since her illness began, she left a doctor's office with hope.

On the ride home, she relayed to her mother what the doctor had said. When her mother failed to respond, she continued.

"Mom, I think it's time I went home to my boys."

"Are you sure you're ready?" Laura asked.

"No, but if I'm not ready now, I'll never be."

"I won't let you leave with any pills of any kind."

"Mom, if that makes you feel any better, I'll wait. I am to slowly reduce my meds every day for a week. Then we'll throw the bottle away together. Don't worry…now I can't stand the thought of swallowing pills."

"Dear, I'm glad we didn't lose you." For the first time in the whole ordeal, Laura had tears in her eyes.

"Me too," Diana replied. "Rich says he'll take me back home when I'm ready. So I'll call him and see if he can take me next week, after I've taken the last of the pills."

One week later, Diana packed her belongings and waited for the black Volkswagen to crest the hill and take her home. When it finally arrived, she looked at her mom, who was shaking her head as if in disbelief. "It's a miracle. We still have you and you are on your way to a complete recovery. You had us all so worried!"

Before Diana left, she handed Laura the now empty pill bottle.

"Here, Mom, throw this away. I don't need these anymore."

"Thank the good Lord," said her mom, smiling.

"Well, ladies, no time for small talk. Rich has to hit the road. Come on sis, before I change my mind."

She climbed into the Volkswagen, placed her two bags in the back seat, and waved good-bye to her mother. In a cloud of summer dust, her mother continued to wave until the car disappeared from sight.

"So…Sis how's your family?"

"Good. Glad I'm coming home."

"You're lucky you have a family to go home to, after everything."

She knew Rich was right, but she felt offended by his comments.

"It's not like I planned for this to happen. I never meant to hurt anyone. Well, I guess no one but myself. But you know, a lot of days I was at Mom's, I felt comforted knowing I had a gun back home," she admitted.

"You what?" he asked, slamming on the brakes and looking at her in amazement.

"Yeah, well, I called it my 'second chance' gun. I bought it at a pawnshop. It's hidden away in a drawer. When I wanted to end it all, I knew if I could just get my hands on that gun, I could…I could…well…"

"Sis, does anyone know you have that gun?" he asked.

"No, of course not. It's hidden in my underwear drawer, wrapped up in a big white napkin. No one would ever look there."

"But sis, you have little kids. What if they got a hold of the gun?" he asked, angrily.

"It's not loaded. But look, I've told you about it. I no longer have those thoughts. Now, I just want to get rid of it."

"Well, when we get to your house, I'm taking that gun. That's not the way I want my nephews raised."

Rich began to cough violently, his hand clenched in front of his mouth, his face grimacing.

He pulled the car over to the shoulder and spit phlegm out the window. His sister turned her head so as not to see. She wanted to shut out his pain, his suffering, but didn't know how. Even when he stopped coughing and continued driving, the sound of shallow breathing and rattling coughs haunted her. The view of her brother on his deathbed spiraled toward her.

A few hours later, Rich turned the car onto the familiar blacktop lane lined with board fences and a pristine row of Bradford pear trees. She tightly grasped the door handle and felt sick to her stomach. Was she ready to come home and face the responsibility of caring for two small children? Diana didn't know, but she knew she had to try.

Rich stopped the car and looked at her before they went inside the two-story brick home.

"Sis, after I visit with the kids for a few minutes, I'm going to excuse myself to go to the bathroom. I'll meet you in your room to get that fucking gun out of your house."

"What are you going to do with it?" she asked.

"Well, I just might take it back to some pawnshop. But you sure don't need that gun anymore."

When they entered the house, Diana found a note on the table from Stuart. He was working late and asked Diana to pick up the boys from the next-door neighbors. Diana decided to wait and pick up the boys after she gave Rich her hidden pistol. As planned, when Rich went to the upstairs bathroom adjoining her bedroom, she took her luggage up to her room. When he knocked on the door, she let him in. Gingerly, she pulled the gun out of the drawer, still wrapped in a white linen napkin.

He checked the barrel to make sure it was unloaded and then placed it in his satchel and went quickly down the stairs.

"I'm getting ready to go see my boys. I can't wait to give them a hug. Will you stay and visit with them?"

"Maybe next time, Sis. I've got to get out while I can. Hope I don't get arrested for carrying a concealed weapon."

A few minutes later, Rich said his good-byes. He seemed inches from her face, his eyes gazing at her intently. "Sis, it's not going to be easy. But you can do it. You have so much to live for."

"So do you," she said.

"Just like I told you, I'm going to keep putting one foot in front of the other, until I can't anymore. Bye, sis."

And he was out the door.

"Call me soon," she replied.

She wanted to tell him she loved him, but for some reason the words stuck in her throat. In a flash, Rich was gone, his black car disappearing in the night's shadows.

Just as Rich said, Diana's life wasn't easy. Feeling weak and drained, it took all of her strength to care for her children and maintain her home. She went to different doctors to determine why she was tired all the time, why she kept getting infections. But they all said the illness was in her head. They kept asking her the same questions. Are you having marital problems? Are you depressed about something? And if she mentioned the plight of her brother, they gave her a prescription for antidepressants and sent her on her way. In defiance, she tossed every prescription into the nearest trashcan.

Rich called often, but she didn't see him for months. One day, right before Thanksgiving, he showed up at her door, smoking a clove cigar.

"Whatever are you smoking that nasty cigar for?" she asked him.

"You have to admit it smells good," he replied with a grin.

Rich was probably the only person who knew how she loved the smell of cloves. It reminded her of making apple butter. As children, Diana and Rich took turns stirring the copper kettle, adding cinnamon and cloves to the apples as they cooked.

Diana knew there was a reason for his visit, but she didn't ask him any nosy questions. He managed his life on his own terms, in his own time.

"Sis, this is my last Christmas," he stated bluntly as he smoked a clove cigar by the fireplace.

"Are you sure?" Diana gasped, choking on the words.

"Yeah, well, that's what the doctors say, based on my blood work."

"How much time do you have?" she stammered, fighting back tears.

"He wanted to tell me, but I told him I didn't want to know. I told him that I, not he, would decide how much time I have."

Unlike his sister, Rich always seemed to be in control.

"Rich, I went to see this new doctor. She actually believes me when I tell her something's wrong. She says that viruses can do all kinds of things to people and that they're hard to detect sometimes. I also talked to her about you."

"Now, wait a minute, sis. My life is my life, and your life is yours. Leave me out of this," he said angrily. The veins in his neck turned purple with rage.

"Let me finish. Rich, she sends her patients with HIV to Mexico for treatments. She says it's helping extend their lives until maybe some better treatments come along. She says she thinks she can help you."

He looked at her in astonishment, seeing the love in his sister's eyes.

"Rich, I'm not wealthy, by any means. But I'd spend every penny I had if I thought it would help you," she said tearfully.

"No, nothing but vitamins and healthy food is going in my body. No experimental drugs, no new doctors, understand?"

She could only nod, tears rolling down her cheeks. He gazed at her, looking deep into her loving eyes. She stared back at him in adoration, wanting to memorize every line on his face, every feature about him. For eternity, she wanted to remember his pale-blue eyes and his crooked smile, smoking that clove cigar by the fireplace.

The holidays came and went, first Thanksgiving and then Christmas. Shortly after Christmas, her brother came for another visit. She couldn't believe how well he looked.

"You're looking great," she said.

"A helluva lot better than you," he replied.

"Well, I've been poked and prodded in every place possible. But this new doctor, she says that my blood work looks like I have some chronic virus in my system. She's gonna start some sort of experimental treatment…with antivirals…to try and help me get better."

"At least you have a treatment option," he replied dryly.

After a strained silence, he continued. "Sis, I'd like to take your boys for a day, if that's OK with you. I want one day to spoil my nephews. How about today?"

She smiled and got the children ready for a visit with their uncle. Hours later, they returned, with ice cream dripping off their collars and clutching multicolored balloons.

"We went to every ice cream store, every toy store in this little town, and bought every balloon we could find," her brother exclaimed.

The two boys were squealing in delight, watching the balloons float above the strings held tightly in their clenched fists.

She invited Rich in for tea, but he declined.

"I've got places to go and people to see," he joked, and disappeared without a good-bye.

The next time she saw Rich was a few months later. It was an unusually warm day in March, and she was outside with the children when she saw his car enter her driveway. His eyes met her gaze, and she was still amazed by how good he looked. For a second, her mind drifted to a recent phone conversation with her mother.

Earlier in the week, she had attempted to tell her mother about Rich's deteriorating condition.

Her mother had replied, "There's nothing wrong with that boy. He's more able to work than I am. He couldn't have AIDS."

Then her mother quickly changed the subject.

She shook the memory of her mother's phone call out of her mind. While her two boys played in their bedroom, she invited Rich into the kitchen and brewed a pot of coffee.

"This is a nice surprise, Rich. You look great!" she added.

Then she noticed the Band-Aid on his right arm and a cotton ball held in place underneath.

"Well, sis, I may look all right, but the doctor says that my blood counts are really low. There's not much left to fight off infection. And, I've…well, I've been forgetting things lately, like what I just said or did. But maybe I've just been distracted."

She started crying. "I'm gonna ask you one more time. This doctor I'm seeing...the treatments haven't helped me much, but she still says she can help you. Won't you even consider it? I don't want to lose you. You're my best friend."

"Nothing but wholesome things in my body. No, sis. Thanks, but no."

"Come and live with us, Rich. If you're sick, I'll take care of you," she pleaded.

"Hey, I didn't drive all the way down here to have a pity party. I want to have some fun with my sis and my nephews. Let's talk about something else."

They sat and talked for a few hours, reminiscing about old times, fun times they shared growing up. Then, as usual, Rich hastily said his good-byes and was gone.

A few weeks later, she was planning a visit to see her brother, when the phone rang.

"Beware the Ides of March," said a dramatic voice on the phone.

"Rich, where are you?" she asked. "Are you on your way here?"

His voice sounded strained and distant. "No, not today."

"Well, I was planning on visiting you next week, if that's OK."

"No, I'm coming to see you soon," he said unconvincingly.

"Well, when? What day are you coming? I miss you."

"Oh, I'll be in touch. By the way, sis, I've been thinking...did you know that time and space are infinite?" he said.

"Yes," she replied, not knowing where the conversation was going.

"Well, I didn't. I was thinking about this today. I knew that space was infinite, but I didn't know that time was."

"So what's making you such a philosopher today?" Diana asked. "And you sound really distant. Where are you?"

"Well, I'm at a friend's house, just visiting for a while," he responded. His voice sounded hollow.

"When will I see you?" she asked again.

The silence on the line was disconcerting.

"Um…soon," he replied.

"Rich, do you need anything?"

"No, sis, I'm good. See ya."

She wanted to tell him she loved him, but for some reason she respected his distance and refrained from the words "I love you" she was already forming with her open lips. "See ya," she replied and hung up the phone. When she heard the line disconnect, she whispered, "*I love you so much, Rich*" to the hollow silence in the dark living room.

———

The phone rang the next day around four thirty as she was preparing dinner. She answered it, hoping to hear Rich's voice. Instead, she heard one of his closest friends, Tim, mutter words she never wanted to hear.

"Your brother's been involved in an accident. I hear it's pretty bad."

"Is he OK? Is he gonna be OK?" she implored.

"He's in the hospital. That's—that's all I know. I'll be praying for you. And for-- and for Rich," Tim stammered.

She called Stuart at his office to tell him the dreadful news and to make arrangements for the children. Then she drove the four hours to the hospital in North Carolina, her mind a blur. She knew how fast her brother drove and assumed he had wrecked his car.

She arrived at the hospital emergency room expecting the worst. But nothing prepared her for what she had to face. When she identified herself, she was escorted to a small waiting room with her mother and sister, Tanya. One look at their distraught faces conveyed the severity of Rich's injuries.

"Where is he?" she asked as she entered the room.

"He's being transferred to intensive care. But before we can see him, the doctor wants to talk to us. We've been waiting for you to get here," said Tanya.

"Is it that bad?" Diana asked.

Her mother did not respond, and wept inconsolably.

"I knew it. I knew it," Diana lamented. "He always drove too fast."

"Sis, he was in the car. But he didn't have a car accident. He shot himself in the head," whispered her sister.

"No! No, this can't be happening. He wouldn't do that," Diana shrieked, then dropped to her knees in shock.

"We have to be strong. Where there's life, there's hope," replied Tanya, pulling her back to a standing position.

The room appeared to darken, and the walls started closing around her. Diana wanted to scream, to run, but she had to face the truth. She had to see him again.

A doctor in sterile white attire arrived in the doorway.

"I want to prepare you before you see your loved one. Rich has a massive gun shot wound on one side of his head. For all intents and purposes, his life is over. He is being kept alive now by a respirator. It's just a matter of time. Of course, sometimes these situations linger. If that happens, you may be faced with the decision of whether to remove the respirator. I don't know who would be making that decision. I assume it would be his mother."

For some reason, Diana felt angry with the doctor for telling them what they'd see, what they should do.

"No, I was the closest to him; I would know what he would want in that situation," she interjected. Diana was ranting like the crazed woman she'd been accused of being. "And you can't tell me he has no chance of survival. My brother is strong. He might pull out of this yet."

"Miss, I don't know how he survived the initial gunshot wound. He is brain dead. It's just a matter of time, probably at the most, hours. But I'll let you see him now, if you're ready," the doctor said firmly.

The three women were escorted through the hospital corridors to intensive care. In the corner of the room lay a gaunt, young man in isolation. He looked like an AIDS patient, his skin drawn tight over his bony cheeks, tugging for his breath. Deep inside, Diana knew Rich was trying to prevent this fate.

In the opposite corner of the room lay her brother. When she first saw Rich, he looked fine on the right side. He appeared peaceful, as if taking an afternoon nap.

Then she saw the gaping hole on the left side, all bandaged. A front tooth was missing where the bullet had entered his mouth.

Tears began to fall down her mother's face.

"He always had such beautiful teeth," wailed Laura, half dazed in grief. "Now look at him, my baby. How could he do this to me, to us?" Her mother sobbed uncontrollably.

Diana stared at her brother's immobile body, draped by machines, and wondered if he knew she was there with him now. Then she began to cry. Only she thought maybe he could hear her, so she stopped. She held his hand and told him how much she loved him. And then, for some strange reason, Diana grabbed his knees with both hands. Growing up, people always said she and her brother had legs shaped exactly alike, down to the same knobby knees.

That night, Diana and her sister and mother kept a constant vigil by his bedside. Around two o'clock, the nurse on duty told them they should go home and get some rest. According to the nurse, Rich could linger for hours, or even days. So, reluctantly, they left and went to her mother's house, just a few miles from the hospital. Around four in the morning, they received a phone call. Rich was dying. The family needed to arrive quickly to say their final good-byes.

Whey they entered Rich's hospital room, his breaths and heartbeat were shallow and irregular. Diana stroked his hair and kissed him on the cheek for one last time. Then the machines sounded an alarm, and his chest heaved. She thought he was struggling at the end to live, to somehow erase the irreversible damage the bullet did to his brain. Abruptly, the waves on the screen went flat.

"I'm sorry. He's gone," the nurse stated serenely.

Diana left the room in a hurry, not wanting to see his cold body. Right now, she didn't want to be consoled by her mother or her sister. She wanted to know why, how, but she wanted to sort things out for herself, on her own time. Reflectively, she thought about the last phone conversation with her brother. Why hadn't she seen through his comments about space and time being infinite? Now she understood why he'd been so vague when he talked about seeing her again.

Her brother's funeral arrangements blurred the next few days. Her mother told people he died in a car accident, and the family upheld her fabricated stories. Thus the family secret was secure—the wayward gay son who was secretly dying from AIDS didn't commit suicide. Better to say he died in a car.

Over time, Diana would piece together her brother's tragic last days. Rich had visited his mother the week before, throwing hints he needed a place to stay, someone to care for him. But Laura had ignored these subtle pleas for help. As Rich drove away from his childhood home for the last time, he rolled down the window and shouted something. But his final words to his mother were inaudible, smothered by the humming car engine.

On the day he died, Rich was housesitting for a friend who was away on vacation, a house on a rural country road in North Carolina. In the house were several shotguns, with plenty of ammunition. But he chose to use Diana's gun with the pearl handle. On the morning of March 19, Rich climbed in the front seat of his car, placed Diana's gun in his mouth, and pulled the trigger. The back pocket of his jeans stored the last of his money, a neatly folded five-dollar bill.

The family decided to cremate Rich's body and have a private ceremony on Laura's property. The funeral was held on a cloudy March morning, two days after his death. But in the middle of his service, the sun broke through the clouds and warmed Diana. She felt this was a sign from him; he was trying to reach her.

After the service was over, Diana was the last to leave her mother's house.

"Before you leave, I want you to have this," Laura whispered.

Laura went to a drawer and pulled out the gun with the pearl handle and the five-dollar bill spattered in blood.

"Why? Why do you want me to have this? Are you trying to make me feel even more guilty than I do? Why didn't I see the signs, when he called me the day before he did this? Why didn't I go to him?" Diana lamented.

"Child, we didn't want to see the signs. I kept believing nothing was wrong with him, because he looked so healthy. I didn't want to face the truth that my son was dying. But we don't know how he suffered. He used that gun to be close to you. Diana, don't you see? There were all kinds of guns in that house, but he used yours."

Laura sobbed, rambling in her thoughts and words. "I can't throw this money away, but I can't keep it either, all stained in his blood. Take them both," her mother shrieked in anguish. "The last time I saw him, why didn't I take him in?"

Diana reached out for her mother's hand.

"Mom, don't keep blaming yourself. For those who understand, no explanation is necessary," she said, her brother's philosophical words reverberating from her own lips.

Hastily, she left her mother's house knowing she couldn't help her mother with her guilt. Diana had too much of her own.

On the way home, Diana took a detour and drove on the back road where her brother ended his life. In her mind, she recreated his last hours, wondering what his last thoughts were before he pulled the trigger. She sat there in silence for hours, feeling his despair, reliving his pain.

While driving home, she subconsciously scanned for black Volkswagen cars. Once, she thought she saw him driving past her in a small town, his arm out the window, smiling. People had told her sometimes the dead return to comfort the living. Maybe that *was* him.

————

A few days later, Diana was alone in her house, wishing she could talk to her brother. She wanted to know why. But then again, deep down she knew. Of all people *she* would know.

Standing on a chair, she reached for the handle of her highest kitchen cabinet and cautiously scanned for the contents inside. Hidden in the back, wrapped in a white linen napkin, lay the gun with the pearl handle and the bloodied five-dollar bill. Diana cried as the guilt flooded her. Why was she still alive and he was gone? She nervously rubbed the pearl handle, knowing that holding this gun and pulling the trigger was the last act her brother had performed. Then suddenly, she heard a noise in the house, little more than a faint whisper of a wind that made her shove the gun back under the layers of white linen and jump off the wobbly oak chair.

Maybe it was just a breeze that blew through her house two days after her brother's funeral. Even though all of the windows were closed and the front door was locked and bolted shut, there had to be a rational explanation for what happened. Perhaps, as she wanted to believe, it wasn't a breeze at all, but her brother's second chance at reaching her, telling her he was all right. Maybe time and space *were* infinite. The breeze only lasted a few seconds, long enough to blow papers off her kitchen table and move the lace curtains in a flutter. Then the breeze was gone and the house was still.

The next afternoon, as streaks of sunlight filtered through her kitchen windows, Diana knew what she alone must do. She took the gun with the pearl handle and the five-dollar bill stained with her brother's blood from her kitchen cabinet. Tightly, she encircled the white linen napkin around them and walked outside. Standing in her backyard, she held the gun over her head for one last time, pointing it toward the sun. Then she dropped the gun and the blood stained bill in the hole she'd dug and buried them deep where no one would find them.

She still didn't know why she'd been spared, why she was granted a second chance. But Rich would have wanted her to make the best of her life, and that's what she planned to do. Diana turned away from the darkness, now buried where it couldn't reach her ever again. Putting one foot firmly in front of the other, she walked onto the clearly marked pathway toward her home.

www.ingramcontent.com/pod-product-compliance
Lightning Source LLC
Chambersburg PA
CBHW020628250626
47154CB00004B/1718